# WELCOME TO THE SPLATTER CLUB III

EDITED BY:
# NIKKI NOIR

ISBN: 978-1-940250-63-2

This book is a work of fiction. Names, characters, business organizations, places, events and incidents either are the product of the authors' imaginations or are used fictitiously. Any resemblance to actual persons, living or dead, events or locales is entirely coincidental.

Artwork by John Wayne Comunale
    www.johnwayneisdead.com

Interior Layout by Lori Michelle
    www.theauthorsalley.com

Printed in the United States of America

First Edition

Visit us on the web at:
www.bloodboundbooks.net

# TABLE OF CONTENTS

# A GRIEVING PROCESS

## CHASE WILL

**P**AUL'S GIRLFRIEND HAD been dead for almost six weeks when the lump in his chest became too apparent to ignore. Up until that point, every pain he'd felt had been psychosomatic, a product of heavy grief mixed with copious amounts of alcohol.

*'It's going to hurt a lot, what you're about to go through,'* his father had told him. *'Be prepared for it. It'll be like nothing you've ever felt, and damn if it won't nearly kill you.'*

He sat in his Pontiac in a strip mall parking lot, staring at the doors of the doctor's office and smoking cigarette after cigarette. His fingers tapped against the steering wheel. The radio was off.

The trip had been challenging. Cruel, really. Here in the city, you were lucky if you made it two miles in under twenty minutes, a far cry from Sandusky, OH, where miles and minutes were often interchangeable. But at rush hour in Columbus, your schedule for the day was at the mercy of the slow-moving deluge of cars. He'd only worked the occasional maintenance job in the city limits, preferring to stay outside the hideous onslaught of bad manners and shitty people whenever possible.

He knew before getting in the car what road he'd have to take. There was no shortcut; it had to be the road he dreaded most, the one where it had happened.

In his mind, he heard the familiar nightmare sounds of shattered glass and Maria's brief scream. The scream, of course, had been cut off by a sound like a stake being driven violently through a slab of meat. And that's all she and their unborn child were by the time Paul lifted his head from the steering wheel—a slab of dead meat, pierced straight through by a deer's antlers.

His father had said it was "no one's fault." But Paul knew, deep down, it was *his* fault. Maria was damned from the moment she fell in love with him. The deer was just an unfortunate catalyst in their destiny together.

*'Death doesn't court the Wascheski clan,'* his father had said, following the accident. *'Only the outsiders. Only the ones we love enough to let in. But there are ways around Lady Death . . .'*

Seeing the park bench—that's what had really pulled a mental heist on him. He thought of the time he and Maria sat on that same bench after making love in a public restroom at *Bar Tabitha* down the street. His arms wrapped around her waist, feeling her warmth against his chest as she looked up at him, passing a cigarette back and forth between their lips. *It's crazy,* he thought, *the things you remember when they're gone.* Specific times that certain things occurred, down to the minute. Odd smells. The way his cotton t-shirt felt against his skin as she yanked it over his head in a quick and carnal frenzy of flesh.

She was dead. He knew this was true, no matter what delusions his dreams tried to plant into his mind. But her grave was in his heart.

And it was a grave she would soon rise from.

He went into the office and sat some more, watching others in their various states of misery. Part of him wondered: *Why not them? Why did he have to be the one to take such extreme measures?*

A nurse called his name, interrupting his dark thoughts, and Paul followed her down a short hallway.

"Step on the scale, please." He obliged, and she nodded, writing his weight in her chart. "Two fifteen. Not unhealthy."

"I was only two-o-five when I was at the Urgent Care a month ago."

"Weight fluctuates, nothing to worry about. What were you there for?"

"Breathing troubles. They said there was nothing wrong. Recommended maybe I stop smoking."

"And are you still a smoker?"

"A fiend."

She wrote this down.

"Any change in eating habits?"

"I don't eat."

"At all?"

"Rarely, I mean."

He followed her further down the hall into a small exam room.

"Any problems sleeping?" she asked after closing the door. "Night sweats, anything like that?"

He shook his head. The nightmares were so frequent nowadays that they weren't even a problem anymore. He got to see Maria. Sometimes the real her. Sometimes the bloodied shell of her.

"And you're here about a lump, correct?"

"Yes."

"May I see it?"

He nodded toward the floor and lifted his shirt up. His left pectoral muscle bulged outward, and the nurse's immediate facial reaction told him the abnormality was as grotesque as he'd imagined.

She put a glove on and gently touched the lump with her thumb. "When did you begin noticing it?"

"Almost three days ago," he said. He added, "I was visiting my girlfriend's grave."

The nurse pushed her lower lip out in what he assumed was a display of empathy.

"I'm sorry to hear that. Do you have cancer or tumors in your family history?"

"None."

"Do you exercise frequently?" the nurse asked. "I'm not feeling anything out of the ordinary. It could just be an overstressed muscle rather than a growth. Maybe you pulled something at the gym?"

He shook his head and watched as she continued writing on her notepad. He needed more time. If he could stretch this visit to an hour, perhaps he'd have the help he desperately needed . . .

"I was wondering," he said. "Is there any way we could do an X-ray? Or maybe an ultrasound, just to be sure?"

"If the doctor thinks it's necessary." She offered a small smile, though, and added, "We typically only do ultrasounds for pregnancies."

"Yeah."

*Soon*, the lump told him. *Be patient, babe.*

He answered the rest of the nurse's routine questions before she left the room, and then he sat there in silence, waiting for the doctor. The lump over his heart kicked like a fetus. It brought a momentary smile to his face.

He'd been to visit Maria's family two days ago. They were still in shock, just as he was, and Maria's father bared his grief in a choked voice that sharply defied his well-built hulking mass. Guilt stabbed at Paul's gut. He loved the man nearly as much as he'd loved Maria. He'd loved her whole family, and the only fortunate thing to come out of the whole situation is that Lady Death had decided to spare them all and only take her. They'd been kinder to him than most people ever were, even with his patchy employment history and farm boy roots.

It made what he'd had to do next that much worse.

*'If you're going to see it through, which I'm neither condoning nor disapproving of,'* his father had told him. *'You're going to need to get to her ashes somehow. Switch 'em out with something similar so they won't notice she's gone. You're gonna want to keep them pure, alright? Don't spill any on the floor. Get as much of her as you can.'*

He'd unlocked their bathroom window from the inside when he'd excused himself. Maria's parents didn't have the luxury of home security, so getting inside the house later than night and making his way to the mantle had only been a matter of patience and silence. Part of him had prayed for his own failure. So many things could go horribly wrong: one wrong move could make a noise that would wake both parents, and her father could come into the room with a shotgun and fire as soon as he saw a shadowy figure switching out his deceased daughter's ashes.

But everything had gone according to plan. He was ashamed at the efficiency of the burglary.

And he'd had a gun with him. He didn't want to do anything with it, and the thought of aiming it at someone he loved made him sick. But he would've done it. He would've shot his to-be father-in-law dead if it meant getting those ashes.

The plan could still go wrong. It could be that he'd done these horrible things all for nothing, and the process would fail him the same way it had failed his father when Mom had died of cancer. This could all be still just in his head, another product of horrible grief leading to sheer delusion.

But his Mom's death hadn't been sudden, and it wasn't due to any sort of curse. Cancer ran in her family, and she'd gone the same way her own mother had gone, slowly and terribly, with all the time in the world for goodbyes. The process his father described to him was said to have only worked once in the entirety of their bloodline, and that was generations ago, the sort of ghoulish tall tale that everyone in the family knew but few actually believed.

Paul was ready to believe anything, though.

He could still imagine the taste of Maria's ashes.

The doctor entered the room. He was a man of slight build, maybe five-foot-six and skinny as a rail. He had a grandfatherly smile, though, the kind of smile that spoke of a lifetime's experience in false alarms and sending patients home to restful nights.

"Mr. Wascheski," he said, extending a frail and liver-spotted hand. "I'm Dr. Barker."

Paul shook his hand, and the doctor looked at his clipboard. The lump in Paul's chest kicked again, as if in excitement. The time it was rather painful, and Paul clenched his eyes. It was getting close.

"The nurse tells me you've been having issues with a lump over your heart. Is that correct? Strange, but not alarming. These sorts of things are rarely what our worst imaginations tell us they are. But good on you for doing your due diligence."

"It's been bothering me a lot," Paul lied.

"Well, let's have a look, shall we?" Dr. Barker said.

He pulled up a chair, and Paul shed his T-shirt. It was the same shirt he'd worn the night of the accident. If the shirt wasn't black, Maria's bloodstains might've been visible to the doctor. But they were hidden. The stench could be attributed to wearing the shirt since swallowing the ashes. Three days without a shower. Three days without food, and only rainwater to quench his thirst. The process demanded it.

"Well, that doesn't look so bad," the doctor said, leaning forward and adjusting his glasses as he touched the lump with gloved hands. He looked a bit like a haggard Santa Claus. It seemed oddly appropriate, considering what he was unwittingly about to do.

"It hurts a lot," Paul lied again. "My chest feels tight. It's hard to breathe. I've smoked for years. Maybe it's lung cancer."

"No," the doctor said distractedly. "This isn't lung cancer. Could be a tumor, perhaps. I'm a man who likes to cover his bases and take every precaution before sending a patient home. Some people think we only do X-rays to crank up the bill. Can you believe that? Makes us out to be monsters. But if it's okay with you, Mr. Wascheski, I do think an X-ray's in order."

Paul hid his excitement.

"If you really think so," he said, sounding resigned.

*'You're going to want to get yourself into a doctor's office when the time comes,'* his father concluded. *'You'll need help delivering, if all goes according to plan. Tell 'em whatever you have to if it gets you into a hospital. Make up something.'*

The doctor gave Paul a gown to change into and left the room. Paul stripped, and as he was putting on the gown, he pitched over with a loud yelp, clutching his chest. He stood awkwardly hunched over, breathing shallow and biting his lower lip in pain. He really felt the kicking now; it was nearly time. The X-ray would keep him here long enough, and they'd have no choice but to help with the delivery.

He practiced his breathing, keeping himself as calm as possible. No time to freak out. No time to rethink what he'd done or contemplate the repercussions.

He stepped outside the room and followed the doctor to the X-ray suite.

Paul's body felt heavier by the second, like he was suddenly carrying an entirely separate person within. His body's shape didn't change, but he knew something within himself was rapidly changing. This was real. The process was working, and they would all see it come to fruition.

The doctor handed him a heavy sort of lead blanket.

"Hold this over the right side of your chest," he said, adjusting the machine. The X-ray camera was a giant square thing resembling something out of a mad scientist's lab. Paul knew from previous experience that the lead blanket was meant to deflect radiation from internal organs, and the thought made him almost chuckle.

*Oh, Doc, if only you knew . . .*

"Hold still," the doctor said. Paul obliged.

The camera quietly clicked.

"Now turn to your right."

Again, Paul obliged, head filled with excited thoughts as he felt the lump in his chest practically pleading with him now. It sensed cameras. It knew the time was close.

Developing the pictures took only a moment, and Paul waited anxiously as the doctor studied them. He looked suddenly dumbfounded.

"That's . . . " He hesitated and reaffixed his calm smile before looking back at Paul.

"Is everything alright?" Paul knew it wasn't alright. He knew it was pretty goddamn far from alright, actually. He was only surprised the doctor wasn't tearing his own eyes out at the sight.

"Maybe you'd like to take a look," the doctor said, motioning him closer. Paul smiled and walked toward the wall, where the two photos were displayed against a glass light fixture illuminating the results.

Almost everything about the chest looked perfectly natural. Strong bones.

But there was a circular blob where Paul's heart should've been, just below the lump. Paul looked at it in wonder.

His grief incarnate. The portal to the other side of death, opening wider and wider within Paul's body.

"It seems there's been a malfunction with the machinery." The doctor turned toward Paul, looking like a man forcing himself to remain calm. "Let's try it again, shall we?"

"Do you have a scalpel in the room, Doc?" Paul asked anxiously

"Pardon?"

"A scalpel. A tool for cutting. Anything like that?"

"Umm . . . Yes." The doctor stared at him questioningly, head slightly cocked.

Paul nodded and stood before the camera. The black mass was pulsing within him again. He'd bided enough time, and now he just needed to pray the doctor would see him through what came next.

"Stand still again, please," the doctor said.

The camera clicked.

As if on cue, Paul fell to the floor, holding both hands over his heart. Pure, beautiful agony tore through him as he writhed on the ground screaming, making sounds that had never escaped his lips until now.

"What is it?" the doctor asked as he rushed toward him. "Mr. Wascheski?"

Paul tore the shirt from his body again, staring down at his chest as the lump throbbed as if someone was knocking from within. The shape of a hand pushed against the inside of his flesh.

*It was actually happening!*

The doctor didn't even scream. He just stared, wide-eyed, as he backed up until he was flat against the wall.

Like pus from a zit, a small finger suddenly shot from Paul's nipple in a burst of blood.

"Help, dammit!" Paul screamed, spreading his own arms wide and practicing the quick breathing methods he'd watched in delivery videos. He screamed again as the rest of a small hand pushed its way out from the hole with a sickening sound, followed quickly by a long and blood-soaked forearm.

The doctor froze in pure shock. All color washed from his face as he watched the small arm flail wildly from Paul's chest. The next moments were crucial; Paul knew he would die if the doctor didn't help deliver his beloved.

"She's . . . coming!" he panted. He was blinded by tears now, tears of joy and pain, both rolled together in strange ecstasy. "Help!"

The doctor moved as if in a trace, wide-eyed as he rushed from the room and hurried back with a scalpel. He knelt over Paul's chest, wiping away blood with the sleeves of his white coat and pressing against the expanding orifice in Paul's nipple.

"Try to stay calm." The doctor's voice was nearly a whisper, hardly audible over Paul's growing screams. He heard the sound of others entering the room, drawn in by the commotion. He heard a man shout a loud expletive before vomiting on the floor.

"Breathe, Mr. Wascheski," the doctor said. The arm reached toward him, as if beckoning for freedom.

The scalpel cut into Paul's flesh, opening the hole wider, slicing through fatty tissue and lean muscle. The top of Maria's head emerged, blonde hair matted over her eyes.

He heard someone in the room fall over. An alarm blared somewhere in the distance and frantic footsteps echoed around him..

"*Keep cutting!*" Paul commanded. "*She's almost out! Keep cutting!*"

The doctor obeyed, allowing the hole to stretch wider and wider as Maria continued to push itself out. Paul breathed, pushing with all his might, nails digging into the floor as he held on as if for dear life.

Finally, Maria's entire frail form exited his body. She crawled across the linoleum floor, leaving a crimson trail in her wake.

She was rail-thin, hardly even recognizable as a human, bones like toothpicks beneath her skin.

The doctor scrambled away on all fours, screaming madly as alarms continued to blare. More people ran into the room and quickly exited upon seeing the monstrosity hugging its legs to its naked chest. Paul ignored the commotion around him as he stared through tears at his beloved, reaching toward her with one hand.

He soaked up one last look at her perfect green eyes before he died.

And that one last look was worth it all.

Chase Will loves punk rock music and all things horror-related. He's the host of The Family Fright Night Horror Podcast, and he's written for several horror websites, including Dread Central, Scare Tissue, and CryptTeaze. You can find him lurking at www.ChaseWill.com

# THE CUNNING LINGUIST

## C.M. SAUNDERS

**THE MUSIC SEETHED** and pounded, the heavy bass lines rumbling in his gut. Standing at the bar with a drink in his hand, Jessie scanned the crowd. It was opening night at The Outer Edge, the newest and shiniest fetish club on the circuit. "Where fantasies become reality," as the marketing spiel said.

These places were all full of bold claims, which was only to be expected. No club would go with something more realistic like, "Come to our place, pay an exorbitant entrance fee, buy some overpriced drinks, and go home and do the nasty with someone you wouldn't look at twice in the street."

The crowd was as much as you'd expect; thirsty older guys, probably married, with bulging waistbands and wallets, and flirty, thirty-something women with needy, desperate looks in their eyes. The men just wanted to fuck someone, then walk away, and most of the women said they wanted the same.

But Jessie had been around long enough to know different. It was deeper and more complex for women. It was never as straightforward as having no-strings sex just because they felt like it. There was always some ulterior motive lurking somewhere in the background. Some craved the attention, some wanted revenge, and others were just damaged. Terrified to commit, but equally terrified of being left on the shelf. Often, the love of one man just wasn't enough, and they wanted to be loved by every man they met.

Someone brushed past and tapped his elbow on the way. It felt deliberate. Like a signal.

Jessie turned to see a tall, skinny guy wearing a leather vest, a dog collar, and a gimp mask with the zip open to expose a pair of red, pouty lips. Probably a bank manager or something.

Without saying a word, the gimp put his hands behind his head, revealing matted armpit hair dripping with sweat, bent at the knees, and

THE CUNNING LINGUIST

began grinding his crotch against Jessie's thigh. He could feel the man's throbbing erection rubbing against him. He was completely out of it. Probably on ecstasy or MDMA. The eyes behind the mask gave the game away; the overlarge, dilated pupils pointed in different directions. He would probably be just as aroused had he been humping a fire hydrant.

Definitely a bank manager.

Jessie smiled and gave the gimp a gentle push, who took the hint and melted away into the crowd. He'd had experiences in his life, but Jessie wasn't really into guys. He was a proud cunnilinguist. His Twitter handle, and his screen name in the chat groups he frequented, was The Cunning Linguist. It was a nice little play on words, but while he might be cunning, he was by no means skilled in languages. Most people understood the veiled reference and knew immediately what his kink was.

He was into eating out, giving head, muff-diving, carpet munching, chewing clams, drinking from the velvet cup, sucking cunt. Or, to give it its proper name derived from the Latin words for vulva (cunnus) and 'to lick' (lingō), cunnilingus. Hence the cunnilinguist, and The Cunning Linguist. It wasn't rocket science. Neither was actually doing it. Though to listen to some guys talk, you'd think it came close. The truth was, the average man was mystified by vaginas. Too many moving parts. And as far as most guys were concerned, going down on one was a chore. Especially after the honeymoon period was over in a relationshit. Something they had to endure before they could get what they wanted, or a necessary evil their wives or girlfriends demanded on birthdays and special occasions.

But to Jessie, it was pure joy. He must have gone down on over a hundred women in his life and hoped he would be fortunate enough to go down on a hundred more. A thousand. He didn't even demand sex in exchange. Sometimes, he just got dressed and walked away, leaving his latest conquest writhing on the bed begging to be fucked.

He didn't mind getting red cheeks, either. It was a deal-breaker for most, but to Jessie, a touch of blood was the cherry on the cake. Like putting salt on his fries. He remembered reading somewhere that earning your red wings has been part of the initiation into certain biker gangs since the 1960s. The Hell's Angels even give you a patch for it. Still, he mustn't get his hopes up. The blood was a bonus rather than a requirement. All he wanted was a pussy to lick. If it happened to be bleeding, all the better.

Obviously, as far as fetishes go, being a dedicated cunnilinguist was pretty tame. Probably even below choking and using anal beads on the list of common perversions, and not even in the same ballpark as something like acrotomofilia, which sounded like a corruption of 'tomfoolery' but was actually the word used to describe people sexually aroused by amputees. What the hell, right? It was just body parts. Or the lack of body parts.

He motioned to the well-groomed bartender and pointed at his empty glass.

"Same again?" the bartender asked, raising his voice to be heard over the throbbing music.

"Sure."

The bartender took the glass, dropped in some crushed ice and a shot of vodka, then filled it two-thirds full of coke. It was somehow refreshing to see that even though the club was sparkly new and no-doubt being crushed under a multitude of health and safety regulations, they didn't insist on giving you a clean glass with every drink. Not yet, anyway. It was bad enough you couldn't smoke inside any more. When every drink you bought came in a warm glass tasting of dishwasher detergent, it really made you question your life choices.

Jessie reached into his back pocket, retrieved his wallet, and opened it.

Suddenly, a soft, warm hand closed over his. Looking down, he saw pale skin and slender fingers ending in fiery red nail varnish, which reflected the pulsating neon lights. Then a husky, though undoubtedly female voice said, "Put your money away, honey. I'll get that."

"Well, thanks very much." When someone offered to buy you a $9 drink you didn't argue, you accepted and asked questions later.

He turned to face this unexpected benefactor, not sure what to expect but preparing himself for the worst. Attractive women didn't need to make the first move, not even in fetish clubs.

He was pleasantly surprised to find a slim woman in her mid-to-late twenties with waist-length dyed blonde hair wearing a short, figure-hugging black dress and heels.

"My name is Cindy," the woman said, holding out her hand.

Of course it was. And her surname was probably Sweetness or Starstruck. Classic porn star moniker, though not quite as cringe as Misty Peaks or Lorna Lust. People enjoyed the freedom assuming a fake name allowed them. It was like being someone else for a night.

"I'm Jessie. Nice to meet you," he said, putting on his best neutral accent. He didn't know whether to shake the proffered hand or kiss it, and in the end settled for a gentle squeeze. "Thanks for the drink, Cindy."

"No problem, Jessie," the woman purred, eyeing him up and down.

Her face was thick with make-up, and there was an angel with wings tattooed on her right collarbone. There must be a story behind that. No doubt she would share it with him later. They usually did. One thing everyone loved talking about was themselves.

All things considered, this woman looked surprisingly normal. She was playing that demure, innocent card so well, and certainly wasn't the kind of girl you expected to find in a place like this. She also appeared to be alone. Maybe she'd found her way in here by mistake.

"So, what do you think?" Jessie asked. As he leaned closer to make himself heard over the music, he detected the faint aroma of . . . what? Lavender? It wasn't what you'd expect a woman her age to be wearing, but it kind of suited her.

"Of what?"

"This place. The Outer Edge. It's opening night."

Cindy shrugged. "Seen one, seen 'em all."

"So you're not new to the scene?"

"Do I look new to the scene?" She giggled, covering her mouth with the back of her hand.

"Actually, you kinda do."

"Well, I'm not."

Jessie wanted to ask what she was into. What floated her boat. He couldn't deny he was attracted to her and could sense his feelings were reciprocated. All that remained was to find out if they were . . . compatible.

But for some reason, he held off. He didn't want to come across as too keen. Besides, he liked the element of mystery. It was exciting. Right now she was just Cindy, and the possibilities were endless. The moment he found out what her fetish was, she would cease being Cindy and become 'Cindy who's into eating poop out of a dog bowl with her hands tied behind her back' or whatever.

Instead, he resolved to make some small talk, turn on the charm, and see where it led.

He didn't have to wait too long to find out. Before he'd even finished his drink, Cindy leaned in and whispered, "Do you want to get outta here? Maybe go somewhere more private?"

Did he ever. Jessie checked his wristwatch. It was shortly after twelve. A little early to call it a night, but if the lady wanted to leave, he wasn't going to try to talk her out of it. He might miss his chance and spend the rest of the night looking for a replacement while she just hooked up with the first guy she talked to who *did* want to leave early. He wasn't about to let that happen.

"I know just the place," he replied.

"Oh yeah? And where might that be?"

"My apartment. It's a fifteen-minute cab ride away."

Boom. There it was. The killer line. And it worked like a dream. He was usually reticent about taking chicks back to his apartment. Once, he'd woken up in the morning to find he'd been cleaned out. His wallet, credit card, phone. She'd even taken his laptop. At the very least, afterwards the chick would know here he lived and might one day decide to pay him an unannounced return visit.

But this just felt right.

Cindy hesitated for just a moment, her left hand going to her hair while her big green eyes gazed searchingly into Jessie's.

What was she looking for? Comfort? Reassurance?

It was at times like this, the women in these places usually expected the man to take control and show her who was boss. He waved his phone at her and pointed at the exit.

*I'm going outside to make the call.*

Cindy nodded eagerly and put her drink to her lips.

Jessie's actions had two objectives. Firstly, he really did need to go outside to call a cab. He couldn't hear a damn thing above the music in the club. Secondly, it would give Cindy a cooling-off period. If she had second thoughts about going home with him, or if she was one of those weirdos who got their kicks from building guys up then knocking them down, it would give her the opportunity to quietly slip away.

If that happened, Jessie wouldn't go looking for her. Nobody liked confrontation in one of these places. It drew all kinds of unwanted attention. Instead, he'd just cancel the taxi and move on with his life.

However, when he came back, Cindy was still waiting for him patiently at the bar. When she saw him, those big green eyes lit up, and they clicked their glasses together wordlessly. By that point, all the talking had been done.

Jessie had got lucky. The taxi company must have had a car in the area, because five minutes later, he and Cindy were sitting in the back seat, fumbling around like a couple of horny teenagers.

Back at his apartment, Jessie was on his knees, ready to pray before the pink altar before the door had even closed behind them. Cindy pressed herself against the wall and sighed deeply when he pulled down her cute little white panties and then opened her legs slightly.

She was shaved. Completely shaved. And judging by how smooth she felt against his cheek, very recently. Probably earlier that same evening.

He couldn't resist an exploratory sniff. It was too dark to see any discoloured discharge leaking out of her that may indicate a nasty yeast infection or an STD, so his nose was his early warning system. He made the sniff obvious. And then did it again. It was surprising how many women got turned on when they knew you were sniffing them. Thankfully, apart from the faint smell of lavender, all he detected was a faint musky odour, a classic sign of a healthy vagina.

It was a green light.

A quiver of excitement passed through him and his heart rate quickened as Jessie commenced licking. Softly at first, the tip of his tongue tentatively probing the delicate folds of flesh as they opened before him like a spring flower.

Cindy moaned and ran her slender fingers through his hair, pulling gently, guiding him. He flicked his tongue expertly against her clit and instantly felt her shiver and stiffen simultaneously.

"Oh God," she sighed. "Do it to me."

Jessie wanted to reply, but couldn't.

His mouth was full.

Instead, he tilted his head to the side and increased the pressure slightly. He often heard people joke about the elusiveness of the clitoris, which was weird because he always found it hanging out in exactly the same place every time.

Cindy responded by opening her legs wider and moaning louder, gripping his ears with her petite hands to hold him in place and rocking gently back and forth while she ground herself into his stubbled lower face.

She was wet now, her juices mixing freely with his saliva as he tongue fucked her into a frenzy.

Jessie thought about relocating to the bedroom, then dismissed the idea. It was more exciting doing it here against the wall. There was something impetuous and unrestrained about it. Like they were living out a scene from a movie.

His dick was as hard as glass, pressing against the unforgiving fabric of his jeans, and he couldn't resist rubbing himself a little with his left hand while kneading Cindy's ass cheek with his right.

After giving her clit and labia his full attention, he slurped hungrily, slowed his pace, and refocused his attention on Cindy's hole. The entry point. This was a definite highlight for him, second only to the complete loss of control at the end when they rode the waves of orgasm. He heard her gasp as his tongue entered the soft, gently undulating tunnel. This was it, the moment of surrender he so craved. He was so turned on he was on the verge of cumming himself.

Then his tongue brushed something not-so-soft.

He paused, frozen mid-action. Was there something inside her? Some foreign object that had been buried deep up her vagina all night and was only now working its way loose? Given they'd met at a fetish club, he couldn't rule anything out.

No, that wasn't it. Whatever this was, it wasn't hard in a wooden or metallic sense. It was firm, but yielding. It was something organic, like a vegetable.

His next thought was that maybe she was having some kind of localized muscle contraction. A woman's body was a complicated piece of kit, and prone to all kinds of unexpected behaviour when in the throes of orgasm.

But she wasn't cumming. Not yet. Not even The Cunnilinguist was *that* good.

Jessie was dimly aware of her thighs gently closing and clamping shut, locking his head in place. But at that moment, he was more concerned with whatever was inside this woman's vagina.

After retreating slightly, he probed again with his tongue, this time a little deeper. His appendage definitely seemed to be touching some kind of fleshy protuberance.

What was that? Some kind of growth or genital wart?

If it was the former, Cindy might not even know it was there. Fuck, he hoped it wasn't the latter. Those things could spread, and the last thing he needed was a face full of warts.

Then another possibility reared its ugly head.

It might be cancer.

The Big C.

He should mention it.

Right now?

If not now, when?

*Yeah, I just thought I'd mention that although I'm no doctor or anything, I think you might have cancer of the snatch. How do I know? Because I was just licking a tumour.*

But again, the conclusion didn't seem quite right.

It was difficult to determine with any degree of certainty using just his tongue, but the little hard lump didn't seem to be attached to the vaginal wall. Or anything, come to that. In fact, it felt more like he was licking the tip of something, something that seemed to reach right up into the vaginal canal and maybe even the uterus.

What the fuck could it be?

Nothing in his education had prepared Jessie for this, and he was torn between being repulsed and consumed with curiosity.

Then it moved. Whatever it was. This thing inside her twitched as his tongue passed over it, seeming to sense he was there.

That's ridiculous.

Ridiculous or not, Jessie decided enough was enough. He'd had his fill of weirdness for one evening. In fact, after this experience, he might even consider changing his Twitter handle to Mr Vanilla.

He withdrew his tongue and tried to move his head, but Cindy held him fast with her hands and knees. She was still moaning.

Arms flailing uselessly at his sides, he tried to say something, articulate his displeasure. But all that came out of his mouth was a muffled exclamation. He was trapped with his face stuck on this woman's pussy. Now, the fluid was literally running out of her, slathering his entire face.

Just then, as Jessie wriggled in an effort to dislodge his head, something snaked its way out of Cindy's still-open vulva and into his mouth.

*What the fuck?*

As the slick, wet protuberance forced its way past his lips and down his throat, his mouth was filled with a bitter, sour taste and Jessie found himself paralysed with shock. He gagged involuntarily, his body trying frantically to reject this invasive foreign object, but it was no use. He could feel it probing inside him, exploring, working its way down his oesophagus like an intelligent, living organism.

Eyes wide with terror, Jessie gripped Cindy's ass with his hands and tried to wrench his head away, but still she held him tightly.

As a last resort, he tried to close his jaws, thinking if he could bite down hard enough, he could sever this thing, whatever it was, before it choked him to death.

Squeezing his eyes shut, he sank his teeth into it.

There was some give, but he couldn't penetrate the outer layer. It felt like thick, puckered skin. But beneath the skin was something with the consistency of fish bone or cartilage, and when Jessie bit down hard, he felt his front teeth splinter.

In desperation, with his broken teeth still embedded, he tried to thrash his head from side to side like a dog chewing a toy. But Cindy still held him. He could feel her fingers splayed out on his head like tentacles.

Whatever was invading him was thick and muscular, tapered to a point, and had ridges along its sides.

It was forcing his mouth open wider and wider.

Too wide.

He let out a muffled cry of pain and despair when, with a jarring crunch, his lower jaw dislocated.

The snaking appendage was in his stomach now. He could feel it in there, writhing and rooting around as if searching for something. In his mind's eye, he saw it travelling along his intestines, pulling, stretching and ripping as it went.

Then there was a white-hot, searing pain as something inside him ruptured. He spluttered and coughed as hot fluid rushed up his gullet and out of his mouth. He didn't know if it was vomit or blood. It didn't really matter.

And then, with something approaching relief, his bowels let go. It felt as if there was simply no room inside him for anything else and whatever was already taking up space had to be expelled at any cost.

The stench of blood and excrement filled the room and Jessie felt his body go limp. It was too much. The shock, the trauma, the pain, the lack of oxygen. It all combined to make him woozy and nauseas.

Now Cindy's vice-like grip was the only thing holding him up, and still the proboscis worked, pushing and pushing ever forward until the tip, the thing he had been licking just moments earlier, protruded triumphantly from his anus. His sphincter widened and stretched to accommodate it, and then split, spilling shit, undigested food, blood, internal organs, and bits of intestine all over the floor of his apartment. Now it was Jessie's turn to moan. But this was a moan of surrender rather than pleasure.

The long tapering trunk-like thing suddenly withdrew, ripping and tearing as it went. At the same moment, Cindy finally relaxed her grip and let Jessie slump to the floor in a puddle of his own filth.

His insides were ruined. He could feel bits of himself leaking out of his orifices. Beyond the physical trauma, he felt violated and humiliated. Used and discarded.

"W-what are you?" he gasped through a mouthful of broken teeth.

"What am I? I'm leaving. That's what I am."

The last thing he heard was Cindy's voice, no longer addressing him, the tone calm and relaxed. "Yeah, I'd like a taxi, please. My destination? Yes. I'm going to The Outer Edge."

When unconsciousness finally came, Jessie welcomed it.

Chris Saunders, who writes fiction as C.M. Saunders, is a writer and editor from south Wales. His fiction has appeared in over 100 magazines, ezines and anthologies worldwide including The Literary Hatchet, Crimson Streets, 34 Orchard, Phantasomagoria, Dead Harvest, Burnt Fur and DOA volumes I and III. His books have been both traditionally and independently published, the next release being the Wretched Bones: A Ben Shivers Mystery, on Midnight Machinations, an imprint of Grinning Skull Press. For more information, visit his website or stalk him on social media:

https://cmsaunders.wordpress.com/
https://twitter.com/CMSaunders01
https://www.facebook.com/CMSaunders01

# LADY TORMENT

## JAY WILBURN

**W**INSTON GARLAND WAS sad when his father died back when Winston was thirteen, but he was absolutely devastated with the loss of his mother twenty-one years later, even before he watched the videotapes of her secret life. Both deaths had been surprises.

His father passed from a massive heart attack before he was forty. A cold man, hard to love sometimes, but his income was certainly missed.

As Winston leaned over a box of his mother's clothes he had just finished stuffing full, he bowed his head and cried again, wetting the polka-dotted pattern of the dress folded on top of the heap. His breathing shuddered as he forced the top on and set it aside.

This would be easier with help and there were plenty of people who loved his mother from church and from the neighborhood who had offered, but Winston had begged them off. He couldn't hold himself together enough to have anyone else around.

He lifted out another box of old video cassettes that he set down with a clatter next to the other four. He hadn't even found a VCR in her house to remotely justify holding on to these. They had to be movies or shows recorded off the TV at some point in the distant past, sometime in the last century, even before his father died.

Keeping home movies might make more sense, but for the life of him, Winston couldn't remember a single moment of a video camera at any family gathering or event. Maybe stuff from before he was born?

The labels were all series of numbers and letters. They didn't even seem to be dates. Could these have been from his dad's work that she kept all this time? How many instructional or training videos did a cannery line manager need? His job was probably replaced by robots by now, and not even smart ones at that.

A few of the tapes had two rows of random letters and numbers. Most just had a single row.

Winston looked around the mess he'd made of his mother's bedroom with all his haphazard sorting. His eyes and throat stung again as he growled out, "Goddamned motherfucking sorry cunt drunk driver! I hope you get raped in Hell."

He groaned and let out one hiccupped sob. Winston managed to get it under control after that, but only barely contained it.

He had to get out of this room. He stalked downstairs into the kitchen, where he pulled one jelly glass from the dusty box on the counter and half-filled it with tepid tap water.

He had a lot of memories attached to all this packed-away kitchen stuff, but he wasn't keeping any of it. All of it was to be donated or thrown away. He had enough to remind him.

He refilled the glass and drank again.

She'd only been fifty-six. She was aging better than he was. Might have outlived him by decades based on the cardiac history on his father's side. But that fucker Derek J. Ryan had seen fit to end that on a fucking turnpike on a toll road. She had been in the pastor's car with the pastor driving. The preacher was in a coma, but Winston's mother in the front passenger's seat and Ms. Meredith Parker, who was in the backseat, had died. The preacher might not make it either, but Fucking Derek had gotten out fine. The drunk assholes always did.

Derek J. Ryan had three other charges before killing Winston's mother on the turnpike. They included a drunk and disorderly with assault last year and another DWI a few months before that. But he was still licensed at least up until last Tuesday.

Winston gently placed the jelly glass overturned in the sink instead of back in the box. Old habits.

There would be a trial. God knew if they'd finally put him away this time. Probably, but he barely cared. Fuck him. Winston would rather beat Derek J. Ryan to death with a lead pipe than have him serve a day.

He kept looking up the guy's picture on that mugshot site. Just staring at it. More than he looked at his mother's pictures at this point. His round, moon face. That uneven dark hair, close cropped, shaved in a fade on the sides. Eyes sunken in his meaty face. A shitty little mustache any real man should have been ashamed of. Beefy muscle showing inside the orange clothing he wore in the picture on the site. In that picture, Derek had the beginnings of a black eye with other bruises and scratches around his neck.

*You should have seen the other guy*, Winston thought in a disconnected way.

Probably Derek J. Ryan could break Winston in half if they really squared off, but not in the fantasies. In the fantasy, Winston beat him bloody, tore down his orange pants, and sodomized the bastard with the pipe lubricated by the drunk fucker's own blood. Not lubricated enough to spare him from getting torn up by the rough rust on the pipe as it violated him.

"Lead doesn't rust," Winston mumbled.

He wandered through the living room and empty downstairs rooms. There was still so much to do. The house was probably too big for her all on her own after Winston grew up and moved out. Life had a way of expanding to fill all the empty space you gave it.

He thought he might just hire a construction dumpster and clean the place out before he sold it. Fuck donations. He just wanted to be done with it.

This time he imagined Fucking Derek laid out from the pipe beating that started every fantasy. He drove his mother's car slowly over him. Derek J. Ryan was pulped. Winston reformed the drunk driver in his mind, so he could find something to sodomize him with. Just dying didn't seem enough, so it always circled back to violation. Maybe he could knock out all of Derek's teeth and stick his own hard cock in the bastard's mouth. Throat fuck him as he pulled out that stupid fucking mustache hair by hair.

He was going to need to sell her car too once he got it transferred over. It would have been easier if that was the car that got totaled.

Winston took down a family portrait that included his father off the wall of the downstairs hallway. He removed the other pictures that still showed his long-dead father. Then he removed the rest, leaving discolored rectangles where the framed photos had hung for too long. As the portraits grew too heavy in the stack in his hands, he set them down on the floor by the edge of the wall. He'd need to bring a box for these and decide what he wanted to do with them after that.

He started with the beating in his daydream this time and followed that up by burning Derek J. Ryan's flesh with a hot brand. Fucking Derek cried and begged for his life as Winston showed his teeth in the fantasy and in real life. Before he was done, he leveled out the brilliant glowing red end of the hot poker with the bastard's ass and slowly inserted it. It sizzled and hissed as it melted and scorched its way inside. Derek convulsed, but stayed conscious through all of it.

Winston opened the basement door and flipped on the light with a loud clack from the switch. It was carpeted and paneled down here during an era of wood patterns and shag. The place was still musty and dank. Boxes piled high on every piece of furniture.

He sighed. If he opened these containers, there might be old comics and vinyl. There might be school projects and more photos. It would be easier, and smarter, to leave their ancient personal treasures unseen and toss them into the construction dumpster he ordered.

The shape of the basement seemed off. It was smaller. No. Things just seemed bigger when you were . . .

Winston passed the hot water heater and gas heating unit. Another paneled wall and door cut off where the rest of the basement used to be. It matched the other dated materials of the space, but there construction was clearly newer.

Back when this was an open floorplan, this back section had been his father's "workspace." The man came home from managing a line at the cannery to carve wood. The place often smelled of sawdust and dark brown finish. The memories of those smells included the man yelling for Winston not to touch anything.

He tried the new door and it was locked. This area, likely filled with yet more floor to ceiling boxes, would need to be cleared out. God, he hoped the key wasn't on his mother's ring in her purse. At some point, he still needed to claim all those personal items from the address the police gave him. It was in an email. He hoped he hadn't deleted it.

He could break the door down. It was thin, but that might hurt selling the house.

As he walked back through the basement, his foot struck a toolbox under the edge of the couch with a metallic racket. Winston slid it out, opened it, and removed a sturdy flathead screwdriver.

It was weird. She gave him copies of keys to everything from the safe deposit box down at her bank to the padlock on the shed that held the mower and extra hose out back, but not this side room? She might have mentioned having this done, and it slipped his mind.

He worked the blade of the screwdriver between the door and the frame, down to the latch. It wasn't shotty work, but this was not a door meant to hold anything secure.

As he fondled the latch, his mind returned to beating the living shit out of Derek J. Ryan. He dwelled on the strikes. After each downward impact, he swung the pipe back up and over his other shoulder. Winston rolled him to his stomach to expose his bare ass. He spread the cheeks with the fingers of one hand to see the brown ring of his real target. The bastard's ass made a wet smacking noise as it opened up, and Winston prepared to really go to work on him.

The door popped open and swung inward. The fluorescent lights were already on. This place was walled off, but the lights were still connected to the same main switch.

Winston's fantasy melted away in his head as he dragged himself back into reality and tried to make sense of what he was seeing. A black leather massage table sat in the center of the room. Ornate chairs lined the wall. A large dog cage sat in one corner. Some sort of wooden balance beam stuck out on one side. A Saint Andrew's cross was mounted up in the far corner. His mind tried its best to translate all of this into stored clutter instead of a coherent whole.

Along one wall was a cabinet with an old boxy TV. Here was the large VCR. It was old even by VCR standards, with the tape insert popped out of the top waiting to be fed. An old bulky video camera stood on a tripod and aimed out across the room. Its plastic side door was folded open with a forgotten video tape resting inside. He really wanted to believe this place was old and forgotten, but red lights were flashing on all three electronic devices.

There was no sign of Dad's old woodworking, unless that balance beam was his doing. He had usually focused on smaller things.

As he walked slowly into the room, he noticed leather restraints on everything. A few included padlocks. She hadn't given him spare keys to these either.

Walking past the edge of the large television, he stopped in place. Across the rest of the cabinet beyond the television were rows and rows of . . . toys. Dildos, strap-ons, riding crops, a leather "flogger" with a fan of leather strips like a cat-of-nine-tails, and other implements Winston didn't have a name for. He watched plenty of Internet porn—not a lot of prospects in his life at the moment. This level of "play" was not his usual taste, but if you searched the porn sites often enough, you'd eventually run across a little of everything.

Past the TV and toy cabinet, a metal work sink that Winston thought might have been left over from his father's days was full of water. Three phalluses floated on the surface. A film of soap lined the edge of the water.

"Interrupted?" Winston whispered. He glanced at the video tape resting in the open camera. Was this what she was doing before she went out with the pastor and Ms. Meredith? What would they have thought about sweet Mrs. Garland if they ever saw this place? Thank God he hadn't asked for any help cleaning out the house. This would all need to go away quickly and discreetly. No donations from this room.

He let out a nervous laugh that sounded way too much like a giggle. He wiped his face with one sweaty hand. "Jesus fucking Christ, Mom."

Winston lifted the tape out of the camera. Maybe he intended to break it or throw it away at first, but he was drifting through today, even before he found this "dungeon" chamber off the wood paneled and shag carpeted basement.

It had two random serial numbers printed across the label. Winston breathed slowly as he stared at the letters and numbers. These were written in black sharpie like some of the ones upstairs. Others used different styles of pen. But one detail he had missed until now was that they were all in his mother's handwriting. Harder to tell with numbers, but it was true.

His hand shook as he moved to the old VCR and inserted the tape. He took a couple tries to orient it correctly. He depressed it into the machine and it hummed to life. He turned on the TV and hit play.

A man's face backed up from being crammed up in the lens and that face turned into the pastor. Over his shoulder, Ms. Meredith Parker smiled and waved. The pastor started to say something, but then the screen went blank except for a couple dancing lines of static.

This was the end of the tape. A man in a coma and a dead woman had come back for a brief appearance. If he rewound, he'd probably see his mother, not just in pictures, but moving and talking. Was he ready for that?

Winston took hold of an ornate chair and dragged it across the floor directly in front of the TV. He tried to ignore the leather straps. He was close enough to the screen that his mother would yell at him if she were still alive.

He fumbled around and found the rewind button. The pastor and Ms. Meredith danced back into view, moving backward at high speed. The image kept flipping on and off like they had been messing with the camera. Lots of static distortion. More darkness.

Winston hit stop. It took him a moment to go back to a VCR mindset. He barely remembered them from being a kid. He managed to rewind the tape all the way faster without the TV showing the whole thing.

He took a deep breath and hit play. His mom's face filled the screen and he paused it. Winston bent forward over his lap and cried. It felt like forever, but he finally wiped his nose and eyes on his sleeve.

He hit play again.

His mom backed up and Winston's breath caught in his chest. She wore a tight leather outfit with her tits hanging out exposed between the leather straps that held them up pert. As she continued to back away, an opening at the bottom showed her shaved pussy. She was pierced down below and on both nipples. Her hair was pulled up into a severe ponytail on top of her head. She turned around and exposed her bare, plump ass.

Until this moment, he'd forgotten the contents of this room and the implications of it on this tape. The pastor and Ms. Meredith, older than Winston's mom, stood naked in the frame.

"Spread yourself on the table, bitch," Mom said. "You know how."

Meredith straddled the 'massage table.' "Yes, mistress."

"And you, piece of tiny-dicked shit, crawl up there on your belly so I don't have to look at that shriveled noodle any longer."

"Hey, take it easy there."

She grabbed him by what hair he had left and pulled his head backward. "You little fuck. I will drag you naked out in the street and never let you in here again. Is that what you want?"

"No. No, Lady Torment. No, mistress. I'm sorry."

"Fuck your sorries, you punk bitch. Open your fucking mouth and stick out your tongue."

"Yes. Yes, mistress."

He opened his mouth and Winston's mother spit down his throat before Winston could pause it.

He stood up and paced the room. He lingered over the table. He even touched the leather over where Ms. Meredith straddled.

"This was the night they died. Right?" There was no one there to answer. "This was why they were together afterward."

Winston hit stop on the VCR to get the image off the screen. His finger hovered over the eject, but then he pressed fast forward and stared at the blank screen the whole time. The whine of the machine started to pick up, and he quickly hit stop like he was killing something coming to attack him.

He ran his finger over the surface of the eject button before he hit play instead.

The pastor moaned with his face in Ms. Meredith's lap on the table. Looks like he obeyed after all. Mom had donned a strap-on at some point and was driving it in and out of the man's wrinkled ass.

"You better please her or you're going to wish you had. Use your tongue for something other than preaching bullshit for once, because your cock is worthless. Do you understand me, bitch?"

He spoke muffled into Meredith's pussy, "Yes, mistress."

Mom thrust harder, making their flesh slap. He cried out.

"Do you understand me?!"

"Yes, Lady Torment." His licking became audible.

Meredith threw back her head and moaned. She grinded her hips into his hidden face and made her tits bounce with the force of it.

Winston might have gone on watching entranced, but something stung his hand. He looked down as he dropped the screwdriver. He forgot he was holding it and now realized he'd been wringing it in both hands as he watched.

Mom called out from the speaker, "You like me going deep. Don't you?!"

"Yes, Lady Torment!"

"Say it, if it's true."

"I like you going deep, Lady Torment. I like you fucking my sissy bitch ass deep! I'm fucking little—"

Winston hit stop and eject. He snatched the tape as the holder was still slowly rising. Storming out of the room and through the house, he found himself in her bedroom again. He stood a moment, staring at the five boxes of video cassettes.

He tossed the tape of the pastor and Meredith onto the bed before he lifted the first box. The tapes clacked together as he stood there. Where was he going to dispose of them that no one could find? He needed to think this out.

He set them back down and lifted out another tape. This one had two lines of code written in ballpoint pen on the label.

Winston raced back downstairs and started the tape. Another naked man knelt in front of Mom with his head bowed. She wore the same leather getup. The man was not the pastor. His dick was a little bigger than the preacher's.

He fast forwarded with the screen displayed. Another woman, fully clothed in business attire, raced onto the scene eventually.

Winston hit play.

"Tell her," Mom ordered.

"I'm sorry I cheated."

"Not good enough," the clothed wife said.

Winston fast forwarded again.

The man was crying while strapped to the Saint Andrew's cross in the corner. Mom and the wife took turns flicking and slapping his erect cock and purple swollen ball sack.

Fast forward.

The cross apparently swiveled. Mom rolled him upside down at some point. Both women squatted over his upside-down face and pissed on him.

"Say it!" Mom yelled.

"Thank you, Lady Torment."

Stop. Eject.

Winston ran back upstairs. He dropped the second tape on the bed with the first. He selected another with a single line of sharpie code.

In this one, a fat man lay strapped facedown on the leather table. He moaned as Mom twisted something into his ass. Then she started pumping it up with air like an inner tube. He moaned louder and then cried out.

"Jesus Christ," Winston whispered.

*Life has a way of expanding to fill all the empty space you give it.*

She pulled the hair on one ass cheek. "Don't you fucking cum on my table or you're grounded."

Winston thought back to the times he'd been grounded and felt a little ill.

"Yes, Lady Torment."

She pulled hard on the device, stretching the ring of his anus into view.

"You feel those studs in there for your pleasure?"

"Yes, mistress."

"Does it hurt?"

"Yes, Lady Torment."

She started inflating it some more.

Winston ejected the tape and then brought everything down, including the two tapes he'd already watched.

As he sorted through the boxes for his next viewing, he took one out and stared at it. He rose slowly and picked up the first tape. The single line of code on the new tape matched one of the lines on the first tape. Winston started to watch.

Lady Torment had the pastor on the Saint Andrew's cross upside right. She jerked his modest cock with velvet gloves on. She took out rabbit fur and squeezed his dick until the head darkened. Then she flicked his balls a few times.

Fast forward.

The pastor, bent over and tied to what Winston thought was a balance beam, splurted cum onto the floor. Lady Torment took a piece of sandpaper and started working his shrinking shaft some more.

"No, I can't take it. Stop." The wooden apparatus bucked under him, but he didn't get loose.

"If you ever refuse me, we're done. Are we done?"

A pause.

"No, Lady Torment."

"You want me to continue to punish you?"

"Yes, Lady Torment, because I deserve it."

He cried as she sandpapered his limp dick.

Winston was pretty sure that wasn't how BDSM was supposed to work. There were safe words and boundaries. Right? Not with Lady Torment, apparently. Not that day.

He looked for the pastor's code on more tapes.

The next tape had the pastor's cock and balls dark from being wrapped in rubber bands. Lady Torment snapped them as she added more and more.

In the next video, he read his Bible out loud as she pegged him with a veining black dildo.

Winston moved on to other videos.

A crying woman sat tied to one of the chairs. Lady Torment swatted her tit with the flogger while a man licked between Lady Torment's legs.

"Your husband eats pussy good. You don't deserve him. You're a cold fucking fish with a used-up cunt. Aren't you?"

"Yes, Lady Torment."

"Then, watch." Lady Torment whipped her again, reddening the wife's chest. "I want you to see how I suck his cock and how I fuck him like he deserves. You're about to go in the cage like the old dog you are."

"Yes, mistress."

Winston looked for more videos with the same code but found none.

The next video had Lady Torment shitting and pissing in some skinny guy's face and mouth. She pulled out a used tampon and squeezed it out into his mouth. Winston tossed that one aside. There were more with that code, but he passed those over.

The next one opened with a thick guy thrusting between Lady Torment's legs. He was really letting her have it. No humiliation, torture, or punishment. He was just fucking her. Winston wondered if that cost extra. The man choked her and thrust even harder.

Winston was about to eject it when Lady Torment switched it up and put the guy on his back. She started biting his cock and balls. She pinched and flicked his nipples. Here it comes. Winston about to eject it and search for another when the man sat up. Winston hesitated. When reached to stop, he staggered backward, almost knocking over the chair.

The hair, the moon face, that shitty mustache, those sunken shark eyes. Winston moaned until it turned into a throat-rending growl. He slammed his fists into both sides of his head. He lunged forward to stop the video but hit pause on accident. The frozen screen distorted all around, but that face remained, staring down at Winston's mom with his dick in her mouth.

Derek J. Ryan!

Winston held the table to balance himself. Then he jerked away from it, dropping to his knees. He cried and gasped for air. He looked up at that familiar face again and started hyperventilating.

It passed finally, but very slowly.

He shouldn't have been down here. Throwing away all her belongings, sight unseen, was always the right move.

"They knew each other," Winston said in a hoarse voice. "They *really* knew each other."

Would Derek reveal that in court? Would it sentence him to more jail time if it looked premeditated? Was it an attack instead of an accident? Coincidence? Huge coincidence if it was one.

Winston gathered every tape with Derek J. Ryan's code.

That bastard fucked his mom's tits. She bit down on Fucking Derek's cock and wouldn't let go. He kept grinding between her tits with what little give he had left.

"Bite it off, Mom. Bite his cock off!" Winston's voice broke.

Derek moaned. Cum drained out both sides of Mom's mouth.

"No, Mom. No! Not him. God damn it."

She let go of his cock and pushed him to his back. She hovered over his face. He tried to turn away.

"No, mistress. Please," he said.

Winston leaned closer to the screen.

She pinched his nose. He eventually opened his mouth, and she drained the foamy cum from her lips. Then she clapped her hands over his mouth.

"Swallow it," she ordered, "if you want to breathe again."

Winston showed his teeth.

Derek gagged under her hand, but finally obeyed.

She let go of him, but ordered, "Stay right there."

"Yes, mistress."

"You swallow cum good. You practice that in prison?"

"Fuck you."

She slapped him across the face. Winston recoiled, expecting that monster to jump up and hit her back. He just laid there. Winston leaned forward in his chair again.

"I will roll you over and fuck your ass, is what I'll do, shit boy. And you'll thank me for it, if I do."

"Yes, mistress."

Winston growled. "Do it!"

"You're a cum guzzling piece of shit, aren't you?"

"Yes, mistress."

"You like the taste, don't you, shit boy?"

"Yes, mistress."

The humiliation went on for a few minutes.

The next tape had Lady Torment cutting and burning Derek J. Ryan. He complained once and she punched him in the eye for it.

Winston paused the tape and stepped outside the dungeon, where he could get a signal. He pulled up the mugshot though he'd just about memorized it. Black eye. Hashed cuts just out of his orange collar. His mother had done this to him. Was that why it happened?

In the next tape, Lady Torment made Fucking Derek punch himself over and over as she masturbated in front of him. She laid him back and he was wearing a chastity cage.

Winston laughed.

"It hurts, mistress," Derek whined.

She imitated his whine and said, "That's because this one has spikes inside. It's supposed to hurt bad boys who get hard without permission."

Winston leaned forward. He glanced at the toys but didn't see any cages. Eyes back on the screen.

She used a vibrator on the cage. Derek cried. She took out a thin metal rod and inserted it into the tip of his caged penis. The metal started to ring through the speakers of the TV.

Winston picked up the screwdriver off the floor and started gouging at the wood of the cabinet under the TV. "Hurt him. Hurt him bad."

He started to slip into fantasy again. He skipped the beating part this time. He'd never considered violating the bastard's cock before. But now he imagined twisting the screwdriver in and out, chewing Derek's dick up from the inside. Woodchips tore away from the cabinet. Winston grew so hard that his dick ached.

In the next video, she pegged Derek's ass. Winston matched her rhythm, stabbing the air with the screwdriver. She finally pulled out and the bastard shit himself, all liquid and lose. Winston laughed hard. Lady Torment smeared it over his body as he cried. She wiped it in his face, and he shoved her away.

Winston's breath caught.

Derek J. Ryan jumped up and took her by the shoulders. They exchanged words the video didn't pick up. Then, he slammed her into the wall out of frame.

Winston stood and dropped the screwdriver. "Let her go!"

"I'll kill you. I'll fucking kill you for this."

"Won't you miss me, little boy?"

"Cut it out. You've gone too far."

"You're the one who shit yourself."

"I said stop."

"I don't take orders, shit boy. Who takes orders here?"

A pause. Too long of a pause.

"I do, mistress."

"Then, on your knees . . . Not there. I want this on camera, shit boy."

Shit-covered Derek backed into frame and knelt by the table. She walked up to him and opened his mouth with her thumb. He sucked it a little. She parted his lips and inserted the shit-stained strap-on. He gagged, but then relaxed and sucked it clean.

"You're my shit boy. Every time I call you shit boy from now on, we'll both know why."

Winston got another tape and found himself wishing he could tell their proper order.

He fucked her and fucked her. Derek fucked her mouth. He fucked her ass. He went back and forth between her ass and mouth, over and over.

Winston's fists opened and closed.

Lady Torment, covered in his cum, led him to the table by his shrinking dick and strapped him facedown. She moved to where he could see her and put on a strap-on. She wiped some cum off of herself and held her finger out to him. He recoiled at first, but then licked her finger clean without arguing.

She removed the dildo from her apparatus and started attaching a much larger, black, veined cock.

"What are you doing?" he asked.

"Giving you what you deserve, shit boy. You have anything you want to say about it?"

"Yes, mistress. I mean, no, mistress. Whatever you say, mistress."

Lady Torment laughed. She lubed the end with a glistening glob of clear gel and then forced it between his cheeks, no matter how hard he tried to clench.

It was as thick as a baseball bat . . . as thick as a lead pipe.

She railed him until he was bloody and screaming.

Winston unzipped his pants, which relieved a lot of pressure. He started stroking himself with a dry hand.

He rewound.

Derek went ass to mouth on his mom.

Fast forward.

Lady Torment slipped inside him and made him cry.

Rewind.

Fucked her mouth. Fucked her ass.

Fast forward.

Fucked him until he bled and screamed.

Winston's cock burned. He'd scratched himself on the side, he thought. Pumping too hard. He thought about being jerked off with sandpaper. He kept going.

Rewind.

Derek J. Ryan sprayed cum all over her in thick white ropes of the stuff.

Fast forward.

"Giving you what you deserve, shit boy . . . "

Fast forward a little more.

Railing his ass. Destroying his ass. Violating his goddamned motherfucking sorry cunt drunk driving ass with a veiny black cock as thick as a lead pipe while he bleeds and cries.

Winston roared and thrashed in the chair as he blew his load all over the carved-up cabinet and the television screen. He heaved for breath as it ran milky down the set. He hissed as the sore, abraded places on his dick really started to burn.

He found some paper towels and cleaned off the screen.

Winston looked for another tape, something with a different code, but he ended up putting in a new Derek J. Ryan film.

"Let's go, shit boy."

# JAY WILBURN

Jay Wilburn was a prolific writer of horror, romance, YA, and science fiction, with hundreds of stories written and published. He won many awards during his astonishing and remarkable career. Along with his podcast "Matters of Faith", Jay was notable for his Patreon and Twitch feeds. While most writers would see others as competition, Jay saw them as friends and he went out of his way to promote and encourage others. Jay passed away on October 18, 2022, he left an impact on the writing community that will never be forgotten.

# MARCH 3RD, 20—

## JOHN WAYNE COMUNALE

**B**EING POOP-SHY is not a good trait to have if you travel as much as I do. Personally, I don't have the problem, but I know a few who did. The bassist in a band I used to play with a few years back held in his shit for five days until he was in so much pain, we had to spend our food money on the cheapest motel we could find just so he could empty his ass.

Money well spent as far as he was concerned, but a huge waste for the rest of us (no pun intended). He had to scrounge for change under the seats of the van to eat for the next few days, which wasn't much. The upside for him was he didn't have to use the bathroom again until we crashed with some friends later in the week.

Needless to say, I find the self-imposed bathroom ban creates an enormous inconvenience for the person *and* people they're with. Everything becomes about timing their shits so the act lines up schedule-wise with them being in close proximity to a private toilet. I understand it's a mental issue for the afflicted, but one I don't really get as I personally will, and have, shit in a hole in the ground in front of people with no qualms.

My comfortability with using whatever bathroom is available to me at the time I need it does have its limitations though. While I'll gladly sit down next to a stranger for dueling bowel evacuations, this is where the pleasantries end. I'm not there to have a conversation with anyone and quite frankly, don't see what there is to talk about. There are certain exceptions when it comes to dealings, nefarious and otherwise, that require the private sanctity of a bathroom like doing or selling drugs. Many sexual encounters and acts are brokered in certain specific bathrooms, though there, one generally knows what to expect and what they're getting into.

On this particular night of the tour, I was playing at a place called *The*

*Hole*, and it lived up to the name in every possible way. More accurately, it should've been called The *Shit* Hole but there's just no truth in advertising these days. The bar had been around for a while with a reputation for hosting amazing underground shows featuring bands with diehard cult followings who would pack the place.

As much as the owners supported the performing arts, they apparently didn't support performing maintenance or proper repairs to the bar. There was a broken ceiling rafter held in place with duct tape when I'd played there four years ago, and it's still busted to this day. The tape hasn't even been changed. A piece of plywood was nailed down over broken floorboards from a rowdy hardcore show that happened before I'd even heard of *The Hole*, and the entire place smelled of stale smoke and sour beer to the extent nothing short of demolishing the building would eradicate the stench.

Posters from shows throughout the years plastered the walls and ceilings, serving a dual-purpose of covering over untold amounts of holes made by steel-toed boots and drunken headbutts. It was the kind of bar you heard stories about how great it was in the sense of what it stood for and its history in the scene. The people who got it understood how special the place was, and those who didn't were most likely never meant to.

There were no bathrooms in the greenroom at *The Hole* because there was no greenroom, and while I could only speak for the men's room, it left much to be desired. I couldn't imagine the women's was any better. Band stickers and graffiti covered every single bit of space on the walls and stalls, and the smell of human excretion was baked into the room. There was no mirror; it either broke or management removed it before my time, and in its place someone had spraypainted a remarkably detailed and impressive giant penis. Why they chose to depict it wearing a bowtie I'm not sure, but I enjoyed the touch of whimsey.

Two of the three urinals had been ripped from the wall, but people still pissed in the holes left behind further eroding the tile and drywall. There were three stalls, two working toilets, and only one door in the center, which was exactly where I was headed. I'd been sitting at the bar nursing a beer when the sensation hit me, or the *urge* from another source, as it were. Something tightened in my gut and goosebumps leapt to attention on my arms. I went hot, then cold, and then hot again, finding myself drenched in flop sweat. I knew there wasn't much time.

"Uh, I'll be right back," I told the bartender, who nodded without looking up from the glass he was drying.

I walked swiftly, and what I'd like to think was *purposefully,* to the men's room, but despite my quick step and close proximity, I knew it was going to be a photo-finish. I slapped the door open and walked directly into the center stall, unbuttoning my pants, hoping the damn would hold in those last few moments, which it thankfully did.

There was no chance to look down and see what I was walking into, not a moment to even give the seat a wipe; not that I cared at that moment. The warm wet touch of a stranger's piss against my ass cheeks demanded action. Apparently, I had the wherewithal to close the stall door because I found myself staring at the back of it as I began to unpack my guts of subpar alcohol and junk food.

The relief was instant but short-lived. As the storm continued to rage within my GI tract, I knew I was in for the long haul. To settle in, I thought of my phone, realizing I left it in my backpack, which was still hanging from the back of the stool I'd been sitting on.

*Fuck.*

There weren't many people in the venue yet, and while I hoped the bartender would keep an eye on it for me, there was no guarantee. I cursed myself, but there was nothing I could do about it now. I wasn't going to start yelling from the toilet for someone to bring me my backpack. I'm not a psycho.

I hadn't been seated long when another patron plowed through the door. I could see his feet make a B-line for the stall next to mine. He sat on the bowl with the same sense of urgency as me, but he was panting, which made me think the poor guy had to run to make it in time. I'd been there myself and could sympathize, though felt no need to verbally commiserate as per my feelings around bathroom conversations. Although, I did wonder why he'd sat down without dropping his pants first.

"Sorry I'm running late." The voice came from the man in the stall next to me. "It took me a little longer than I expected, but hey, I'm here like."

I didn't respond, assuming he was talking on the phone.

Then he kept going.

"Okay, okay I get it. I told you I'd be on time, but the silent treatment?"

Again, I said nothing.

"Hello? Come on, man."

"Are—are you talking to me?" I said finally.

"Yeah, I'm talking to you, Phil. I know I've fucked up before, but you don't have to be an asshole *all* the time."

"Phil? Uh, no I think you have me confu—"

"I don't have it all on me now," he continued, either ignoring me or choosing not to listen. "Don't freak out though. Do not freak out. I have *most* of it, okay, just not the whole thing. *BUT* don't worry. I just swiped this dummy's bag so I'm sure I can get—"

"Whoa, whoa, whoa," I interrupted. "I don't know who you think—"

"I said don't freak out, okay? I'm sorry. Here, this is what I got. Take it."

I looked down to see the man's hand come under the divider, clutching a wad of money, most of which looked to be single dollar bills. His hand was filthy, and his fingernails were rimmed in black grime.

"What? What the hell is that?"

"Just take it. I know it's not the whole thing, but take it for now, okay?"

"I—I don't want that." I reached down to push his dirty hand back under the divider, regretting it the instant I made contact. "Get out of here!"

He resisted, finally dropping the balled-up bills to the floor, using his foot to push them further into my stall.

"Let's see what else we have here." He rummaged through a bag. "I'm sure this asshole has something you can hock for the rest of what I owe."

The man dropped something on the floor, and I heard the distinct sound of a zipper. I leaned to the side to get a better look and saw my backpack on the disgusting bathroom floor between his legs.

"Can you believe some guy left this on the back of one of the stools? What a fuckin' mark. I mean, how dumb can you be? Man, this is mostly a bunch of junk."

I went to say something but at the same moment, he picked up my bag and dumped its contents onto the floor of his stall. I was too stunned to speak. I went to stand but another surge of bowel pressure forced me back to the toilet.

"Hey man! Hey!" I said after the splashing of my next load stopped sloshing in the toilet. "What the hell are you doing? That's *my* bag!"

"There's a piece of shit phone in here."

He didn't seem to understand what I was saying, and I was in no position to do anything about it as another wave of wet hot heat pushed through my asshole. I cried out in frustration and agony.

"It's not *that* bad," the man said. "I'm sure we can get something for . . . Say. Now, here's a nice little surprise."

I knew what he'd found before I heard him greedily snorting. It was the drugs I'd accidentally stolen ten days prior from a crazed giant named Zeke, then convinced him the punks throwing the house show where I'd played had taken them, but not before I had sex with his girlfriend several times.

"Whoa shit. Woooo! Goddamn Phil, I mean, goddamn!"

I still wasn't sure what drug it was but knew enough to know this was bad news. It wasn't exactly coke, though it looked like it, and was far harsher than most things I'd put in my nose. It burned like a motherfucker, especially if you weren't ready for it, which my stall neighbor, currently robbing me, was experiencing presently.

"Holy shit." I heard him take another toot. "I don't know what the hell this is, but it's stronger than a motherfucker. This right here is worth what I owe you and more. Hell Phil, you might come out of this owing *me* money."

"I told you asshole." I stood, having finally flushed out my intestines, and pulled up my pants. "I'm not Ph—"

The door to the bathroom swung open, crashing against the back wall. The man next to me gasped audibly and tried unsuccessfully to stifle a whimper. I froze, before opening my stall door.

"P-Phil? I thought you—"

"You thought nothin', Craig, you little fuckin' snake. Now, where's my fucking money?"

I got a quick look at 'Phil' through the crack between the door as he stormed forward, lunging for the man whose name was Craig. The glimpse was brief, but he was frighteningly large and solid. Over six feet of muscle packaged in a sleeveless shirt, tight black jeans, and steel-toed boots hurled itself at the man who owed him money while I quietly stepped away from the stall door.

"No Phil, please. Look! I got this . . . stuff for you."

"The fuck?" I heard Phil snatch the baggie away, followed by the distinct sound of his open palm slapping Craig's cheek. "You use the money you owe me to buy drugs from somebody else?"

"No, I fo—"

I imagine Craig was going to say how he found those drugs, and that he did indeed have Phil's money, or part of it at least, though he'd given it to the stranger in the center stall by mistake. Also, how good he thought the drugs were, and that he'd estimated their value to be higher than what he owed. He was able to impart none of those thoughts because the man he wanted to tell them to was currently punching him in the face repeatedly.

The drugs most likely numbed the pain of the first few strikes, but when you're being punched in the face that many times, no matter how numbed you are, you still know you're getting punched in the face. Between blows, Craig moaned and mumbled while Phil punctuated each strike with a well-timed expletive.

The beating felt like it lasted forever and the few times I thought it was over, it would start back up again with Phil switching hands or adjusting his grip. The stall divider shook violently from Craig's weight thrown against it, and the brackets holding it into the wall buckled. I thought it was coming down on me for sure, but the wall held, and the beating stopped. There was more cursing, followed by shuffling sounds as Phil picked Craig up from the toilet.

"We're not done yet by a long shot fuck-o," Phil said. "Let's go."

Through the crack between the door, I saw Phil had slung Craig's arm over his shoulder, holding the man's limp, crumpled form close to keep him upright. They exited the men's room, the door slammed shut behind them, and I was left alone. The hot stink in the air was now peppered with the unmistakable aroma of blood, and I waited a full minute before flushing the toilet, picking up the wad of cash Craig dropped under my side of the divider, and exiting the center stall. The first thing I saw was my mostly empty backpack in the corner where it'd been kicked, along with various articles of my clothing scattered across the floor.

Craig's stall was a horror show, but a scene that would hardly register to the patrons of *The Hole*. Blood spattered the back wall and dripped in long, thin, crimson streaks. A couple of my t-shirts were covered in Craig's blood—those would be staying behind—and I counted two teeth on the floor, though to be fair, they could've belonged to anyone.

The bag of drugs was gone, but luckily my phone was still there and most of my clothes were salvageable. I repacked my bag, washed my hands thoroughly, and returned to where'd I'd been sitting at the bar.

"Oh hey, there you are," the bartender said. "Man, you'd been gone so long, I thought you fell in. Ha ha. Need another one?"

I fake smiled, forced a laugh, and nodded, accepting his offer. I looked around the bar and while it was slightly more crowded, there wasn't much in the way of bustling activity. I saw no sign of Phil or Craig, and nothing seemed out of the ordinary as far as I could tell. There were droplets of what looked like blood on the floor leading from the bathroom to the entrance, but there were similar trails crisscrossing the entire bar.

"Here you go, man."

The bartender set a beer and shot in front of me, and I reached in my pocket, digging out the wad of bills I'd been inadvertently gifted. There were a lot of ones as I'd seen initially, but as I dug through peeling them off to pay my tab, I found a few twenties buried at the center. I paid and tipped the bartender, then inspected closer to find there were more than just a few twenties. There was $460 worth. I don't know how much more this Craig person owed Phil, but I'd guess it was enough that the beating he received was well deserved.

After my set, I was able to buy *real* cocaine from the friendly local dealer who hung out at *The Hole* every night. *And,* while I could afford to buy decent food, I elected to purchase two hotdogs and a greasy slice of pizza from the gas station next to my motel. I wasn't worried about the consequences. The next club I was playing had pretty decent bathrooms.

John Wayne Comunale lives in the neon-drenched city of sin Las Vegas to prepare himself for the heat in Hell. He is the author of *Death Pacts and Left-Hand Paths, Scummer, As Seen On T.V., Sinkhole, The Cycle* and more. He hosts the weekly storytelling podcast John Wayne Lied to You and fronts the punk rock disaster johnwayneisdead. He currently travels around the country giving truly unique and most excellent performances of the written word.

# YOU'RE MINE NOW

## RACHEL NUSSBAUM

"**ALRIGHT, SWEETHEART.** *I need you to stay calm.*"
The voice flowed like a torrent of ice water against Simon's ear. He flailed awake, eyes snapping open to darkness.

He was sore as shit. That wasn't new—his leg was still healing in his cast and he'd sold all the Vicodin the doctors gave him days ago. But this was a different ache. His whole body was tingling, thrumming with heat.

What the fuck had happened? Simon barely remembered parking at the rural address Glenn had sent him to for the job. Everything else was fuzzy. It felt like an atomic bomb exploded inside his head.

Simon blinked again, startled, realizing despite the pitch black around him, wind blew across his face.

What the . . .

Simon felt for a blindfold, wincing when he made contact with his unobstructed eyes. His hands were *wet*.

What the fuck was this? Why couldn't he see? Simon reached out and his palms touched tile floors.

Wet tiled floors. Warm and slimy. Jesus Christ, what the fuck.

"*Calm, remember? It's . . . Simon, right?*"

*Fuck, that's right, there was someone else here. He didn't sound like one of Johnny's regular guys. At least not the one who'd broken his leg.*

"*Hey, hey. Take some deep breaths, Simon. Don't panic.*"

The voice coiled through the darkness, echoing off walls he couldn't see, like whoever was taunting him was all around him.

"*C'mon, sweetheart.*" He was right against Simon's ear now. "*Three deep breaths for me, and I'll let you see.*"

What the *fucking* fuck. Simon swung on reflex, his arm sailing through empty air. The movement made the skin on his shoulders burn.

"Where are you?!" Simon called out, hoarse voice cracking.

"*Three deep breaths first.*"

"I don't have all the money yet," Simon whispered. "Johnny said I had until Saturday, I swear I—"

"*Is that what happened to your leg?*" It sounded like he'd stepped back, giving Simon room. "*Someone broke it because you couldn't pay them? You poor baby.*"

It wasn't one of Johnny's men. What fresh hell had Glenn sent him to now? Simon shuddered out a sob. Or maybe a laugh. He was so fucking exhausted and scared. He dragged in a deep, trembling breath.

"*Just like that. Good job. Keep breathing.*"

"What do you want?" Simon whispered.

"*I don't want to be here. I'll tell you that much. Looks like neither of us had much choice. Didn't seem like you were with the rest of those freaks.*"

Freaks?

"Who are you?" he asked.

"*Okay. Like a bandaid then. Just try to stay calm. This is going to be jarring.*"

Before Simon could ask what that meant, his vision snapped into place. Like someone just reached out and turned on the light.

Everything was red.

The sleeves of his jacket were soggy with blood. Near frozen in horror, Simon looked down at the puddle he was sitting in. It was deep red and warm. Fucking hell, there were *chunks* in it. Simon cried out and pushed back with his good leg, sliding himself out of the puddle and up against a wall.

Simon looked around desperately, his heart pounding in his ears. He was in a bathroom, those disgusting ones at public parks, with a doorless entrance, two empty stalls, and a dripping sink covered in bloody handprints.

It was impossible for all this blood to come from Simon. He'd be dead if he lost even a third of this mess. He opened his jacket, wincing as shredded, sticky skin peeled from the fabric.

He was shirtless under the jacket; his bare chest *mutilated*. Deep, angry gashes had been carved into his flesh. The back of his throat prickled as Simon shed the jacket, examining the length of his marred body.

Symbols. Runes. They'd been etched down his entire torso, disappearing into his bloodsoaked jeans.

Simon's head swam and his vision blurred.

"*No no, darling. Let's not pass out again. Not out of the woods yet.*"

And as quick as he started to lose consciousness, Simon's brain pulsed hot, like he'd touched a live wire. He opened his eyes and lurched forward. Delirious and horrified, Simon looked at the entrance. Then to the empty stalls.

"Where the hell are you?" he said. "How are you doing this?!"

Silence hung heavy in the air. Simon's head slumped, and he stared at his ruined chest. The incisions of the symbols opened and closed with each shuddering breath, and a wave of nausea washed through him.

How didn't this hurt more? Why wasn't he in *agony*? The cuts needed stitches. Some went down to the bone.

Why weren't they bleeding?

Cautiously, Simon sucked in a deep lungful of air, watching his chest expand. A particularly thick gash over his heart parted wide. He braced for pain but barely felt a sting.

Something moved inside.

He spat his breath out with a horrified curse, and the cut swallowed up further movement. Simon waited a moment before inhaling again and parting the gash further. His skin ripped, a single trickle of blood leaked from a wound that should likely kill him. He had to find out what was in him.

Simon's heart stuttered when he saw it clearly. A row of thick, white . . . tendons? Bones? No, they were moving. There were . . . nails—*claws*.

They were *fingers*.

As soon as Simon realized what he was looking at, the fingers wriggled, then retreated out of sight. An eye took their place, peering out at him.

"*Hello.*"

Simon passed out.

When Simon gained consciousness, cold night air blew the scent of smoke across his face. He was in the woods, leaning against a tree.

"*Oh good, welcome back,*" the voice said. "*Had to move you. They caught up to us.*"

"Fuck," Simon whispered, shivering. Why the fuck was this happening? How? Had the jobs finally gotten to be too much and he'd snapped? Or maybe one of Johnny's men drugged him—

"*This Johnny again. Is he also the reason you're missing some fingers?*"

Fuck, it could hear his *thoughts*.

"*Cute.*" The voice chuckled at his realization. "*I'd love to unpack that, but we need to keep going.*"

Simon yelped as he was pulled to his feet by an invisible force. His legs flailed under him, and he winced as his cast scraped the dirt.

"*Ugh, do you mind if I get rid of this? We don't really need it right now.*"

Before Simon could respond, his arms moved of their own accord—reaching down and ripping his cast in half like it were nothing. Panic surged through Simon's mind when his broken leg was lowered to the ground.

"No, wait—"

"*You're alright, darling, I'm holding everything together. Start running.*"

Something pushed Simon and he stumbled forward, bracing for pain. But just like the voice assured him, he felt nothing but bone deep pins and needles. Like his leg was asleep and not broken in two places. The force pushed his back again, and as terrified as Simon was, he leaned into it and started running.

As he ran, the smell of smoke got stronger. He could hear voices nearby. See the flicker of lights in the distance.

*Fire.*

It came through in bits and pieces—Simon remembered being dragged to a bonfire. Trying to break free and getting hit across the head. Waking up naked, hooded figures crouched over him with knives, chanting and carving into his flesh.

Burning from inside. Pain, torment like he'd never felt before in his life, and he'd had two fingers cut off and his leg recently broken with a bat.

And almost as soon as it started, it stopped. He remembered the chants turning into screams and squelches.

"*Starting to come back to you?*"

"What the fuck?" Simon nearly tripped. "What did they do to me?!"

"*Looked to be some kind of ritual sacrifice, yeah?*"

"Who the hell are they?"

"*I was really hoping you would know. I just got here. Context clues, I'm guessing cultists. You know. Crazy people.*"

Simon couldn't believe this. He was having a conversation with a demon inside his cuts.

"They're . . . who we're running from?" he whispered.

A booming laugh echoed in his ear. Something tickled under Simon's scalp. Like his hair was being ruffled from the inside-out.

"*No, Simon. We're not running from anyone.*"

Before Simon could register what that meant, a dull sting in his hands stole his attention. His fingertips were splitting apart, the nails flaking off and skin peeling back. Thick, jagged claws pushed out of the wounds. From the stumps of the fingers Simon was missing, two entirely new digits sprouted. Sickly gray and soaked in blood—the same fingers Simon has seen inside his wounds.

"*Sorry, I'll fix it all later.*"

Simon's body swerved left and he jumped off an embankment. He barely saw the figures below him before he tackled one to the ground.

"IT'S THE VESSEL!"

The hooded figure cried out and Simon felt a disgusting squish and crack. His hands—the claws that had slipped through his fingers—were buried in the man's chest.

Simon gagged. He felt wet tissue and splintered ribs digging into his skin. And just as easily, Simon stood and threw the man's twitching body aside.

Fucking shit, he just killed a man with his bare hands. Simon started to scream, but fingers against the inside of his mouth wrapped around his teeth, swinging his jaw shut.

*"Sorry, sweetheart, but I have to get to the bottom of this. Close your eyes if you like, it won't take long."*

Simon couldn't have closed his eyes if he tried. He watched in absolute horror, helpless as his body was puppeteered. He staggered to the nearest of the two remaining figures. The cuts across Simon's body tingled and multiple rows of sharp teeth pressed against the inside of each gaping wound.

*"What have you freaks done?!"*

There was a snap from behind Simon, and suddenly, *real* pain bloomed through his back—he whimpered under the hand that muffled him.

And almost as soon as it started, it was snuffed out. Simon spun around. The man behind him pointed a crossbow at him.

Did he just get fucking shot in the back by a crossbow bolt?

"You fool!" The other man shouted at his armed companion. "We are not to harm the Vessel—"

Simon's hand lifted and something hot tore through his palm. In the next moment, the man with the crossbow screamed and collapsed, the bolt he had fired into Simon now lodged in his own cheek.

Simon turned back to the other hooded figure, frozen in awe and terror. He cast his own crossbow and torch aside and dropped to his knees.

"My lord," he started. "Mercy, please. We are your acolytes. We serve you."

*"Do you now?"* The unholy abomination spoke from the gashes in Simon's flesh. *"Sure didn't feel like it when you tried binding me with silver chains at your creepy little campfire. Didn't work out so well for the rest of your friends, hmmm?"*

Simon's body stomped forward toward the cowering acolyte.

"Please prince, the ritual hasn't been completed. Your true arrival is just steps away!"

Simon tensed at that—at the idea of more mutilation, more of this nightmare. Fuck, this was too much. He wished Johnny had done him a favor and just killed him like he'd sworn to.

At that thought, the hand wrapped around his teeth retreated.

"*Hey, hey,*" the voice spoke in Simon's ear. "*Don't let this psycho scare you. I don't understand what he's saying either.*"

Suddenly, Simon was tackled to the ground.

"My pain is a cage, it shall not hold me!"

Simon thrashed, looking over his back. He caught a flash of the other acolyte, the eye above the bolt rolled back in his head and nostrils dripping blood.

"Unhand the Vessel." Simon heard his counterpart protest. "The Elder warned not to harm him, you foo—"

The acolyte was cut off and fell to the ground, a series of bolts sticking out of his neck and jaw.

"The Elder prolongs our salvation. He doubted your power and strength, my lord. I am loyal to you, not him."

Simon felt the end of the crossbow press against the back of his head.

"Break free from your own cage, prince of hell! Deliver us!"

"*Brace yourself, Simon. This won't be comfortable.*"

Pins and needles bloomed through Simon's neck, hard and fast. He felt a crack and his vision spun. He was staring down the crossbow now, looking right into the one working eye of the horrified acolyte.

Fucking hell, his head had twisted around.

Simon's jaw unhinged. Scalding hot, viscous liquid flowed across his tongue, spraying the crossbow. Its wood smoked, dissolving as the green slime ate away at it. The acolyte shouted as it reached his hands and his flesh sizzled.

And then another spray from Simon's mouth hit him in the face.

The stream sliced down his nose and the cartilage melted away, snot and blood oozing out. His shouts soon devolved into desperate, wet gurgles.

Simon bucked the twitching body off his back, cleared his throat, and gripped his neck, twisting his head back into place.

"*Well, they were all supremely useless, weren't they?*"

Simon shivered as control returned. He looked down at his hands and watched the claws retreat, the wounds closing up and nails regrowing instantly. An eye poked up against a symbol on Simon's wrist.

"*You alright?*"

Simon shook.

"What the fuck are you?" he whimpered.

"*My name is Yates.*" Simon could swear he felt a hand gripping his from inside his palm, lips being pushed up against the underside of his skin. "*Charmed.*"

Simon had never had it together all that great, mentally. It's part of why he turned to drugs in his youth. For a long time, he thought he might be schizophrenic.

Now, soaking in the bathtub of a lakehouse he'd broken into, watching the tap turn off by itself and a towel float across the room, Simon had an almost worse fear.

"Are you really a demon?" he whispered.

"*Pffft. No.*" The voice—Yates—laughed.

"They said you were . . . a prince of hell?"

"*They didn't know what they were talking about,*" Yates said. "*And there is no hell. Or maybe there is, I don't know. I'm just not from there.*"

Simon's broken leg was suddenly yanked forward. He yelped and wrenched it back against the invisible iron grip.

"*Shhh, relax darling. I'm going to fix this. It'll make everything easier.*"

"Fix it?" Simon echoed cautiously.

"*Yes. Now, first I'm going to let go. It'll feel like how it was before momentarily—focus on that pain. Show me where to go.*"

The blunt ache of his broken bone returned with a vengeance. Simon brought his fist to his mouth, biting his knuckles. Fuck, he forgot how much it *hurt*. How the fuck had he gone over a week with no painkillers?

All at once, the numbing tingle Simon had experienced since first hearing Yates invaded the muscles and bones of his leg. Simon scrunched his eyes shut, bracing for whatever Yates planned to do next.

And suddenly, it faded away. The pain, the swelling, even the dark, angry bruising disappeared. Cautiously, Simon wiggled his toes, rolled his ankle.

"*Good as new,*" Yates said.

" . . . You healed my leg?" Simon asked incredulously.

"*I can heal any damage I do immediately, since I know exactly how to put it back together. Like with your fingers or when I twisted your neck. Other wounds are a bit more complicated. I need to feel the pain myself.*"

"You can *feel* my pain?"

"*Yes. Then I know where it is exactly that needs fixing. I could probably regrow your severed fingers for you, but that might be overdoing it.*"

Simon took a shaky breath, looking down at the open symbols etched into his skin. Looking at them closely, something about them looked vaguely familiar, but he was in no state to place them. Out of the cuts several eyes peered up at him—one from his wrist, one from his stomach, one on his thigh. They were all different sizes, pupils rectangular like a goat. Translucent eyelids flicked over them in tandem. Simon shuddered.

"Can you . . . heal all this? These markings?" he asked.

*"Yes, but I won't."* Yates said sympathetically. *"I have no idea what they are or what they mean. They could be keeping us both alive for all I know. Sorry. While we're on the subject, though, what on earth were you doing with that cult? I saw a bit in your head but not the full picture. You went there willingly."*

Simon sighed and sunk back into the tub.

"I needed money. Someone who finds me odd jobs said he had something. Didn't say what, but he said the payout would be huge. I didn't ask. I just went."

*"He set you up then?"*

Simon was quiet. He'd known Glenn for years. He thought he was a friend. The jobs he'd taken from him were never clean, per se. Drug trafficking. Money laundering. Cleaning up suspicious bloodstains. Simon never asked questions.

He was so *stupid*. He had been texting, begging for work all week. Glenn knew he would show up, he practically served himself up on a silver platter.

Fucking couldn't trust *anyone*.

*"This is all for that Johnny person, yes?"* Yates asked. *"I can see him in your head. You're very scared of him. Dresses nice, lots of tattoos. The one who broke your leg and had your fingers chopped off?"*

Simon looked at the stumps on his left hand. It had been over a year ago, but sometimes he swore he still felt them ache.

"Yeah. I owe him a lot of money." Simon stepped out of the tub and grabbed the floating towel. He felt the cuts in his side wink shut as he dried. Fuck, this was so weird.

*"What a wretch. Would you like me to kill him?"* Yates offered.

Simon's heart stuttered.

"No, Jesus. You've killed enough people for tonight," Simon said firmly.

*"Everything I've done was for self-defense and preservation, Simon."*

"Defense!?" Simon asked, blinking. "You hunted those men down. With *my* body. You made me fucking . . . you . . . seriously you made me—"

*"I was trying to get answers out of them. I'm sorry if that was uncomfortable for you—"*

"Uncomfortable?! You made me crush a man's rib cage with my bare hands!"

Yates was quiet. Seething, Simon grabbed the clothes he'd pilfered from the bedroom. They were big, but they'd work. He slid on the sweatpants.

"*It wasn't all a waste. They mentioned an Elder. Must be their weird little cult leader. Probably who your traitor friend sold you out to, yes?*"

Dread sunk into Simon's stomach.

"*Where do we find Glenn?*"

"No," Simon said.

"*Pardon me?*"

"I don't—I can't take anymore of this," Simon said. "I don't want to go back to the cult. I don't want to hand myself over to their fucking *leader*, of all people. And I don't want to have to just . . . sit in the back of my brain and watch while you use my body to kill people. It's too much. YOU are too much."

"*I'm too much?*" Yates echoed from Simon's chest. He sounded like he'd been slapped. Simon looked down and was met with at least a dozen eyes staring out at him from his wounds.

"YES. YOU'RE FUCKING TOO MUCH," Simon shouted at him.

"*Hmmm,*" Yates rasped in his ear.

Suddenly, Simon's legs buckled beneath him. He slammed to the ground, only to be yanked backward, pulled up so he was kneeling in front of the floor-length mirror. The lights in the room flickering as he strained. Simon opened his mouth to shout, but like before, he was gagged from the inside.

"*Simon, I have tried being courteous. I have tried being nice.*"

Simon's arm shot out. His fingers splayed and a cut appeared, sliding through his palm like butter. A mouth pushed up against the inside of the cut. Jagged, sharp black teeth and pale, dripping gums.

"*I understand this is horrifying for you. It's not ideal for me either, and we are on a time crunch to get this mess sorted. If you're going to be difficult, I can offer you the kind of incentives you're used to.*"

The gashes in Simon's skin began to sting. He stared into the mirror, watching them spread apart. Blood-soaked fingers dotted in nasty claws slipped through the gaps. Dozens. Hundreds.

"*Feel this?*"

Something hot and sharp flared in Simon's head, spiking painfully at the edges. He gagged.

"*The only reason you're not in excruciating pain right now is because I've got a good grip on your parietal lobe. The only reason all your blood is still inside you is because I'm holding it in for you. I always make it a point to be a good guest, but you're not being a very accommodating host.*"

The cuts *hurt* now, definitely not as much as they should, but enough to make Simon close his eyes and whimper.

*"I haven't the faintest idea why or how I'm here, and that makes me very nervous,"* Yates continued. *"For all I know, every minute I'm in here makes this binding more permanent. I don't want to get stuck in this fragile mortal body anymore than you want a 'demon' inside you."*

Simon could feel Yates' hands inside him, claws dragging across his tissue. Fingers twisting across the inside of his throat. The back of his calves. Up and down his spine.

*"Now, this isn't a request—it is an order. Take us to Glenn. I don't want to have to hurt you, but I'll admit it, I would love to see you beg. Hmm?"*

The fingers unclasped from Simon's mouth and he gasped.

"I'll do it!" he yelled. "I'm sorry, I'll do it. Fuck, please, I'll do whatever you want . . . "

The pain stopped immediately. The fingers retreated, and the cuts shrank. The pins and needles washed back over Simon's flesh, and he slumped down and gasped out in relief. As he sucked in air, a single hand patted his back from the inside.

*"Good boy,"* Yates whispered. *"Let's hop to it."*

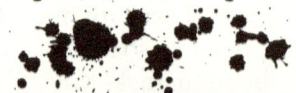

It wasn't Simon's first time stealing a car. It *was* the first time the car started itself for him, though. They were a few hours outside of the city, not too far from where Simon had originally been sent. Yates told him to feel free to sleep on the drive.

Yeah, fucking right, like that was possible.

Simon stared through slitted lids at the moving steering wheel, trying to take a mental stock of all the unholy powers Yates possessed. Aside from being able to break and heal his body at will, he seemed to give Simon inhuman strength. The acid-vomit thing, he remembered with a shudder. He could lift nearby things telekinetically, control electronics, and who knows what the fuck else. Questions thrummed in Simon's mind, and he swore he heard Yates chuckle at his thoughts more than once.

"You never said what you are when I asked." Simon finally said.

*"Are you asking me to tell you about myself?"* Yates sounded amused.

Simon's face reddened at Yates' teasing, but he nodded.

*"There's no easy way to explain that,"* Yates answered. *"In the most simplistic terms, I—we—are from a different plane. Dimension. Reality. Whatever. We've been around a lot longer than your species. Than your planet, really."*

"We?"

*"My kind. We can make . . . portals into your world, to reach through,*

*interact with. Observe. Explore. But our portals need to be anchored to something. A person or at least a place with a lot of human energy attached to it. We can't reach too far from our portal, and our power is limited, but we can move in and out of our world and your world that way."*

"What do you mean by a person or place?" Simon prodded.

*"The most common choice is people, obviously, since they're portable. Older places that have absorbed a lot of human emotion and energy are easy to infiltrate too. Houses. Places of worship. Cars are fun, but it can get weird controlling electronics. Doesn't usually last long."*

"This just sounds like you're describing possessions or hauntings."

*"Ha, yeah."* Yates cackled. *"Humans often call it that."*

"You said you *weren't* a demon." Simon huffed, exasperated.

*"We're not, but humans call us that sometimes. They call us all kinds of things. Demons, the Devil, ghosts, spirits, angels, the fae, God, Jesus, aliens, I could go on. That's all us."*

Simon blinked.

*"I mean, maybe some of it's something else, I don't know,"* Yates admitted. *"But most of it's us. We've been popping in since you crawled out of the primordial soup. Got a bit baked into your mythos."*

"This is insane," Simon mumbled.

*"If it's too much for you, I can take it out of your head—"*

"No, thank you!" Simon said quickly.

Yates chuckled, and something tightened in Simon's chest. He looked down and saw a pair of eyes and a mouth pushed against a wound by his clavicle.

*"It's never been like this before. When we go through our portals, we're not sending our whole selves in. It's like . . . a projection of sorts. We're not corporeal in your world and you shouldn't be able to see us for more than a flicker or two. Not like this."*

Yates stuck two fingers out and wriggled them at Simon to demonstrate.

*"I can't get back into my world, either,"* he said. *"It's like I'm stuck in you."*

Simon swallowed.

"That's fucking terrifying, Yates."

*"Sweetheart, you're not wrong."*

Glenn wasn't home. Yates let Simon pound on his door for a minute before he got impatient and broke the thing into splinters, but the apartment was empty.

"Fucking hell," Simon groaned. "If I had my fucking cell, I could just call the bar and ask if Glenn is working—"

"*What is a cell?*" Yates interrupted.

"Er . . . you know. A cellphone. A mobile phone?"

"*Ohhhh!*"

Simon's arm jerked forward, and one of his wounds flared apart. In the next instant, his phone was being pushed through his flesh, covered in blood and pus.

"YATES WHAT THE FUCK," Simon shouted.

"*Come on, take it!*"

Simon gagged, reached in, and pulled the rest of the slimy phone out of his arm. It passed through his tissue, rubbing against tendons and bone. Jesus fucking Christ this was too fucking gross.

"*I grabbed it back at the bonfire, but I didn't know what it was. Mobile phones looked very different the last time I was here.*"

"When the hell was the last time you came to Earth?" Simon mumbled, wiping the phone on his pants.

"*1994. I also have your wallet and your underwear in here.*"

Simon pretended he didn't hear that, and he pretended that it made sense the phone would still turn on after being stuck in a dimensional pocket inside his arm.

"Blue Moon, how can I help you?"

"Lani, hey," Simon said into the phone. "Have you seen Glenn? Was he working tonight?"

"Simon, shit, you didn't hear?" Lani asked.

Oh fuck, what now? There was a clipped silence as Lani likely stepped into the back of the bar.

"Glenn's in the hospital."

"What the fuck?" Simon gasped.

"He stepped on some toes and got jumped. Beat his ass with a bat and took all his product, too. He's been in the ICU for days."

Simon's blood went cold.

"Thanks for letting me know, Lan," Simon mumbled.

"Sure thing, man. Try to take it easy," she said before hanging up.

*Fuckkkkk.* Simon slumped down against the wall. Glenn hadn't been the one who texted him about the job. He hadn't been the one who set him up.

"*Forgive me if this is presumptuous, but bats wouldn't be a calling card of your friend Johnny, would they?*"

Simon held up his arm and looked into Yates' wide eyes.

"Glenn and Johnny do run in the same illicit circles. Often competing ones," Simon mumbled.

Fuck, if that were true, that meant Simon had been texting a phone Johnny had for days. He'd have seen how desperate he was. That he had nothing to give him.

"*How much do you owe this bad man?*" Yates asked.

"I'd gotten it down to 50K."

Yates was quiet.

"*I don't know what inflation is at, but that's probably still quite a lot, yes?*"

Simon nodded. It was more than he could make payments on lately. If Johnny decided he'd finally been bled dry and wanted to cash out . . .

*Years.* Fucking years of desperate jobs, living between slums or in his car, of handing over every scrap he had. Years of being beaten to a pulp when that wasn't enough. The whole time, this is what Johnny planned to do with him, wasn't it?

"Motherfucker sold me!" Simon shouted, hitting the wall. The drywall cracked. "Like fucking *livestock.*"

"*Simon. You are VERY angry right now,*" Yates noted, his voice honestly surprised.

A pair of hands gripped his shoulders from inside him, rubbing up and down the pockets between his bare muscles and skin.

"*I like it.*"

The night was winding down, and the club Johnny owned in everything but name had just closed.

So Simon didn't ask Yates to be careful when he pried a rideshare bike out of its rack and hurled it through the windowpane. The shouts erupted immediately, and moments later, Johnny's men came running out.

"*You can close your eyes, if you want,*" Yates offered, picking up another bike.

Simon kept them open wide, relishing as Yates took a wheel in each hand and turned to Johnny's men.

It happened in an instant, right as the first of them reached Simon and Yates. One moment, the man was shouting obscenities, reaching for his gun. The next, Yates snapped the metal of the bike around the bastard, like he was folding a piece of paper around a bug.

The loud squish and various cracks and pops stopped the rest of Johnny's men in their tracks. Blood and ground flesh oozed through the gaps of metal and rubber. The bars had crushed the goons' bottom jaw, his breastbone, his extended arm. He spit out broken bits of teeth, still half alive and choking on his own smushed tongue.

Simon tossed the bike—man and all and turned to the rest of Johnny's men. Yates flared the cuts that contained them, pressing dozens of his mouths against the wounds.

*"Who next?"* he hissed.

Simon scanned the group of horrified men, most running, some frozen solid, some aiming their guns. He singled out the one with piss running down his leg. The one who laughed so hard the year before when he cut off Simon's fingers.

"Him." Simon nodded.

*"Your wish is my command, sweetheart."*

The man was wrenched forward to his knees, dragged across the concrete of the road until he knelt in front of Simon.

*"Simon,"* Yates whispered, practically giddy in his ear. *"He has a pacemaker."*

The man raised his gun with shaking hands and unloaded a clip. Simon felt the fire and the sting of each round, but the pain vanished the moment each bullet sank into his flesh, the wounds closing up seconds later. Simon whispered a mental thanks to Yates.

*"Watch this,"* Yates whispered back.

Simon's hand lifted, and so did the finger-cutter, until he was practically floating off the ground, toes scraping the concrete desperately.

The man flailed, screaming, unable to find purchase. His arms twitched in the air, his eyes rolled back, and foam poured from his mouth. Simon's jaw dropped as smoke snaked out of the bastard's chest and the smell of burnt flesh wafted from him.

And then he burst into flames.

"Jesus Christ, Yates!" Simon shouted. The man was burning alive, screeching in inhuman agony under the flames. After a few moments, he pressed the gun to his head.

The shot echoed and bits of brain showered Simon.

*"Aw."*

"Have you ever heard the term over-kill?" Simon mumbled.

He felt teeth trace across the inside of his temple, nibbling at tissue. A cut opened in Simon's cheek, and two fingers slipped out to flick a chunk of gray matter off his face.

*"Am I being 'too much' for you again?"* Yates cooed, fingers stroking his cheek.

Simon shivered.

"You're sick in the head."

*"I'm just teasing you,"* Yates said. *"It's not my fault you're into it."*

"I'm fucking not," Simon said.

*"I'm in your head, darling. You most certainly are."*

Simon stepped over the smoking corpse and made his way to the stupid fucking club, singing a song loudly in his head for absolutely no reason.

Johnny stood from the leather sofa in his office as Simon walked in. Simon could never control the fear that swelled in him when he saw Johnny. Even now, with unholy power, his heart pounded. Years of being dragged into this office. Of being tortured. Of being used.

This time, though, Johnny looked scared too. He looked like he'd seen a ghost.

"How . . . " Johnny trailed off, glancing at his cellphone and reaching for his gun.

"Don't bother. They're dead," Simon said.

"How on earth are you alive?"

Simon scoffed, lifting up his marred arms.

"You sold me to a demon-worshiping cult, Johnny. How the fuck do you think?"

At that, Johnny froze.

"It worked?" he whispered.

And to Simon's shock, Johnny took a step forward.

" . . . My lord?" he whispered. "Are you there?"

What the fuck.

Johnny sunk down to his knees, bowing before Simon.

"Vassago. Prince of hell," he murmured. "We have awaited your arrival."

Oh fucking shit. Panic surged in Simon. His cuts flared as Yates pressed his mouths up.

"*Oh great,*" he spat. "*Another one of you freaks.*"

Johnny's whole face lit up, an expression Simon had seen many times when he was bleeding on the floor.

"Prince of hell, our Church has awaited you for decades—"

"*I'm not Vassago, I'm not from hell, and I killed your Church, you weirdo.*"

Johnny was quiet, his face pinched in confusion. So was Simon's—this fucking mobster was a cultist? It made no sense. He stared at Johnny, trying to slide the puzzle together. His five-hundred-dollar silk shirt, sleeves rolled up to show off his tattooed arms—

His arms. The symbols.

It was like a mirror image of the tattoos carved into Simon. Black ink instead of open red cuts.

Fucking shit.

"You answered the call. You have to be Vassago. Is . . . this a test?" Johnny asked.

"*Ugghhh, don't tell me you're the Elder?*"

Johnny's eyes widened and he shook his head.

"I was his second. I procure funds and arrange for sacrifices and your attempted Vessels. I can't believe this was the one to finally hold you. I would have offered him to you years ago if I'd known."

Yates growled.

"*Don't talk about him like that. Where is the Elder?*"

"He wasn't on the other side?" Johnny asked, face falling. "He crossed over years ago. To prepare you for your arrival."

Dead. The Elder was dead. Simon's heart sank, and Yates glared with eyes that had reached the end of their rope.

"*This is why I killed the others,*" Yates whispered to Simon. "*They're annoying and nothing they say makes any sense.*"

"Do you know how to undo this or not?!" Simon barked.

Johnny glared up at him, sneering. He glanced back down at Simon's cuts.

"You wish to enter our world, don't you Vassago?" Johnny asked. "To traverse our plane unanchored, made flesh? No more bindings?"

Simon glared at Johnny, waiting for Yates to tell him to shut up.

But Yates was quiet.

Oh no.

Johnny smiled.

"That is what I and your acolytes desire," he continued. "Our Church invites you to take your place in the mortal world. We opened the first door for you."

"*And was this a part of your plan, too?*"

Yates waved Simon's arms in the air.

Johnny's delighted laugh chilled Simon to the bone.

"Yes. He is your Vessel. Your . . . pressure cabin, as we invoke you from hell to earth."

"Yates?" Simon whispered.

Yates ignored him, pushing him forward.

"*And how, pray tell, do I get out?*" Yates asked.

Johnny made eye contact with Simon, grinning, bringing his hands together and miming an opening gate.

"Open the second door. Burst forth. We invite you, shed your Vessel and be made flesh at last. Unbind yourself."

*Fuck.* Fucking hell.

Simon wasn't stupid. He knew what was coming next. He knew Yates had only kept him alive because killing him might kill them. This, though, this was it. It was the end. There wasn't a more fitting one for someone like him.

He closed his eyes tight, waiting for it.

"*I reject it,*" Yates said flippantly.

"What?" Johnny spat, brows furrowing.

"*I reject you. I reject your invocation, I reject your worship, and I reject your Church.*"

Yates lifted Simon's hand at Johnny.

"*I like Simon more.*"

Johnny flew back against the wall.

Yates walked his shocked body forward, hand still raised. The lights in the room flickered.

"*Funny thing about me, Johnny,*" Yates said, stalking up to his pinned form. "*I don't particularly enjoy killing people. Not typically. I don't like people who enjoy killing people, either. Especially people who are innocent.*"

"Innocent?!"

Johnny struggled against his invisible binds.

"That Vessel is nothing but a waste of life," he snarled through grit teeth. "Just like all of them. He's a felon and an addict, a drain on society, a stain on the world. I gave him to you, you hear me?! I own him and I gave him to you, prince! To be your door! You cannot reject the call!"

"*Oh, I'll accept him happily,*" Yates said. "*He's mine now. But I reject your call, you freak. I reject your sick ideology and every cruel, evil little thing about you. Tell me, how many people did you psychopaths kill on the off chance you might bring one of my kind to earth?*"

Johnny's hand wrenched to the side, and suddenly, two of his fingers snapped. He cried out before his mouth was yanked shut, screams muffled against his lips.

"*Bite down on something,*" Yates said mockingly.

Johnny's right leg snapped up at the knee. The crack was loud enough that Simon winced.

He winced again at another crack, and when he looked at Johnny's face, blood trickled out. He'd bit through his tongue, cracked his teeth together.

"*I don't usually enjoy hurting people, but you, Johnny? I think there's a special place in your hell for people like you. And when I send you there, it'll be a mercy.*"

Yates held up both of Simon's hands, and Johnny's broken fingers and leg began to spin, the bones cracking further and the skin tangling in circles. Johnny's eyes bulged out of his head. Simon could hear the powdery grind as broken teeth strained against each other.

The bones in Johnny's leg broke through the skin, but Yates didn't stop. He kept spinning the limb, letting the jagged splinters of bone tear through the flesh until they sawed off every string of muscle and tissue. His leg fell to the floor, along with his two fingers.

"Fucking hell, Yates," Simon mumbled.

*"Almost done. Can I add one more touch?"*

Simon stared at Johnny, pinned in torment and bleeding out against the wall. He remembered all the times that had been him, bleeding and begging for mercy in this very room.

"Yeah."

Simon's cuts flared, and several silver pellets fired out. It took Simon a moment to recognize they were bullets, the ones that had been shot into him earlier, filed to sharp points. They fanned out and dug into Johnny's flesh. He flailed at the onslaught, tears and blood and snot running down his face.

The bullets danced across Johnny's arms and legs, twisted around his chest. Simon watched them tracing his tattoos and realized what it was Yates was doing.

*"Eye for an eye,"* Yates said smugly.

The grisly ordeal lasted several minutes, and when it was done, Johnny's clothes were in tatters, blood and pulp dripped down the wall, forming a puddle on the floor. Somehow, he was still conscious—Simon wondered if that was somehow Yates' doing.

*"Now then, Johnny,"* Yates said, letting the bullets clatter to the floor. *"What was it you asked me to do? Unbind myself? Burst forth to the world?"*

Johnny's head lifted, and his eyes widened. He shook his head, cries garbled in his sealed mouth.

*"After you."*

The cuts on Johnny's body splayed open and he lurched forward, grunting. Heaving. The cuts parted further, the flesh inside tearing deeper, through tissue and fat, down to organs and bone. The pulp bloomed outward, curling at the edges as they were flipped inside-out.

His stomach and intestines spilled through the gaps—now more like craters. A loud crack sent Johnny's ribs folding out through the holes in his chest, unfurling like a flower, exposing his fluttering heart, his hyperventilating lungs.

*"I'd leave you like this for a few decades,"* Yates said, stepping forward. *"But Simon said I need to learn about overkill. You're lucky he's so merciful. I wouldn't have been."*

Yates splayed Simon's fingers, and Johnny's torso unfolded against the wall with a splatter. His arms and remaining leg went flying, his head toppling lifelessly to the floor.

Simon fell to his knees.

"*Phew. Okay, that might have been overdoing it.*"

Simon doubled over, dry-heaving. At some point between gasping and gagging, he started laughing.

He laughed so hard he fucking cried.

"*Simon? Sweetheart, are you alright?*" Yates asked nervously.

"Yeah," Simon whispered. "We're alright."

"*Simon?*"

Simon blinked, sitting up from the driver's seat. They'd helped themselves to one of Johnny's nicer cars, seeing as he wouldn't be needing it. They'd also swiped all the material about the cult in Johnny's office, though neither Simon nor Yates could make heads or tails of any of it. Yet. It had been . . . weird, the last few days. Being in limbo together like this.

But it wasn't *bad*. They'd figure it out in time.

"What's up?" Simon yawned.

"*Vassago is a stupid name.*"

Simon laughed.

"Is Yates even your *real* name?" he asked.

"*It's not,*" he said. "*Just a nickname. The first human I ever met gave it to me. If I spoke my true name, your eardrums would probably explode and all your organs would rupture.*"

"Fuck off. Where the hell are we heading, anyway?" Simon snorted, stretching his arms.

Yates sighed in his ear. Simon looked down at his arm, at the faded scars of the symbols Yates healed the day before. A small cut opened at his wrist and an eye peered out fondly at him.

"*The ocean,*" Yates said gently. "*It's always been a favorite. We don't have anything like it where I'm from.*"

Simon couldn't help but smile at that. At this ancient, terrifying being, so content just to make it to the shore.

Rachel Nussbaum is an author and artist from The Big Island of Hawaii, currently living in California. Her dad showed her *Alien* as a kid and she's loved monsters and body horror ever since. Rachel's stories have been featured in previous anthologies from Blood Bound Books such as *Night Terrors III*, *Crash Code*, and *Welcome to the Splatter Club Vol II*. More recent publications of hers include "Adrift", featured in *Cosmic Horror Monthly* #28 and "Starved", published in *More Than a Monster* from Grendel Press. In the future, Rachel hopes to write some full-length novels and illustrate her own stories and comics.

You can keep up with Rachel's writing over on her Instagram: https://www.instagram.com/rachelnussbaumwrites/?hl=en

# SELF-REPORTING

## STEPHEN KOZENIEWSKI

"**Hey, Pop,** there's blood on the walk."

I grimace. Dammit. Henry is home from school early, probably for the first time in his life. The kid had to pick today, of all days, to not linger at the softball field or beg to walk Rosita Hernandez home. No, today he rushes home like a model fucking citizen.

I reach over and grab the shotgun.

"Hi boy," I call out, forcing my voice to assume its normal, chipper timbre. The child must not be allowed to suspect a thing. "Yeah, I saw that. I think the Copes' cat was through here. He must've been in a fight. You know how that damn animal is."

Henry yanks on the screen door. I remembered to lock that, at least. Thank God for small favors. There is no key to the screen door, and Henry bangs on the doorjamb.

"Hey, Pop, the screen door's locked!"

I take a deep breath. I have a moment (and not a split second longer) to collect my thoughts and marshal all my resources. Now comes the hard part. I must get from the powder room where I have been disinfecting and bandaging my leg to the front door without the boy noticing my limp. I tuck the shotgun behind my back, surreptitiously, I hope.

I take a step. White-hot bolts of agony flood my nervous system. I thought I could just tough my way through this, but clearly that isn't going to happen. Okay, only ten more steps to go.

"Pop!" he repeats, pounding on the doorjamb.

Walking without exposing the limp is impossible. I shuffle the rest of the way as best I can and when I reach the door, brace myself with it using my right hand. My left hand is on the trigger of the gun hidden behind my back.

I smile. Try to control my breathing. "Hey, Henry. You're home early."

The boy looks suspicious. No reason why he shouldn't be. He's already seen the droplets of blood on the front walkway. Worse, probably, I haven't let him in yet. He yanks on the screen door as though that will budge it.

"Come on, Dad. My back teeth are swimming."

I nod. Yes. Of course. What kind of parent wouldn't let their child into their own home to pee? But I must get him away from here somehow. He mustn't go near the powder room.

"I meant to ask, can you pick up a gallon of mint chocolate chip from the drugstore? Sorry, I meant to text you before you left school."

"Yeah, okay, I'll go back out," he says glumly. "But can you let me in? I really need to pee."

I purse my lips. What the hell answer can I even give to that? "Um . . . could you get the ice cream first? It's right across the street."

He slams his fist on the doorjamb again. "Come on, Pop! Let me in!"

Flop sweat must be pouring down my face. Doubtless I'm white as a ghost.

"It's just that the toilet in the powder room is stopped up. That's what I was doing when you got here. Trying to plunge it."

Henry rolls his eyes. He doesn't want to hear any more about my constipation than I feel like making it up. Everyone knows what "the toilet is stopped up" is code for.

"All right," he says, "I'll use the upstairs one."

"Don't they have one at the drugstore? I mean, I'm just saying . . . "

"Fine!" He cuts me off sharply. "I'll go across the street. Just give me the money for the ice cream before I pee my pants."

Shit. It really would be awkward not to give the boy money. "I'll pay you back."

"I don't have anything, Pop."

"You don't have five bucks?"

"No, Pop!" He's very agitated now. "I spent my last two bucks on lunch."

Okay. All right. I can let him inside. I won't just give him five bucks. I'll give him twenty with a wink and a nod. He'll spend at least a half hour on a child's equivalent of a spending spree at the drugstore. Maybe he'll head to the arcade and give me another hour or two on top of that, but that could be wishful thinking.

I reach for my wallet, and the shotgun topples out of my hands, clattering to the floor. Thankfully, the damn thing doesn't go off, but the look of horror on Henry's face is no worse than if it had.

"What the heck are you doing with that, Pop?"

I try not to miss a beat. "I was just cleaning it. That's what I was doing when you . . . "

"I thought you said you were plunging the toilet."

There's a note of severity in his voice, too mature for an eleven-year-old. I'm not sure if there's any point in continuing deception. The jig is most likely up.

I try to dive for the shotgun, but the pain in my leg overwhelms me. The door clatters shut behind Henry and he takes off running down the brick walkway. I struggle to lower myself to the floor, eventually succeeding in getting my good knee low enough to scoop the weapon into my cradling arms.

I pepper the screen door with a blast of buckshot. Henry, halfway down the walk, hisses in pain as a few pellets catch his shoulder, but for the most part, he's unscathed.

"Shit, shit, shit," I mutter, breaking the shotgun. A few red shell casings clatter to the floor as I fumble through my pocket, but the pain is too severe to try to reclaim them right now.

I repeat my feculent mantra as I slam the door and bolt it. Then I add a "Fuck" as I sink to a sitting position on the landing. I cradle my leg. The bandage is the familiar consistency of a damp washcloth, but instead of warm water, it is soaked through with my blood.

"Fuck," I repeat.

I could've told the boy I wasn't bitten. He could have looked at the wound with his own eyes. If I were infected, the blood would already be black with sepsis and have the thickness of molasses riven through with yellow streaks of pus. I'm not infected, but that doesn't matter. The rules on reporting are ironclad.

Self-reporting is the first step. Any jagged wound or abrasion that could conceivably have been caused by a bite is immediate cause to report to a local community health center for quarantine, which is, of course, a death sentence. Even if they were fine at the beginning, anyone with a jagged wound being packed into pens with other quarantined people are going to be infected by the end of quarantine. Which provides statistical proof reinforcing the government's quarantining and self-reporting rules. 100% of those quarantined are found to be infected by the end of the week. So self-reporting must be working, right?

And when those with demonstrable wounds fail to self-report, families are expected to report non-compliant family members. Which is where I find myself.

Just last week little Maggie Johnson's mother dragged her, kicking and screaming, to the health center for the crime of falling from climbing a tree and abrading her arm. We'll never see her again.

I'm not sure what my plan was to get through this exactly. I suppose I would have avoided intimate contact with my wife for a while. That hardly seems to be a problem anymore these days. But now even my most outlandish pipe dream has been reduced to a zero percent success rate.

"He's inside."

Shit. Whispering outside. I struggle to my feet and limp over to the front door. Peering through the peephole, I can see Annette standing on the front porch, her face demented by the fish eye.

" . . . shadow over the peephole."

Shit. I wipe a sweat-drenched lock of hair out of my eyes. I raise the shotgun and level it at my wife, unsure how much protection the door will afford her. A bullet would almost certainly punch through, but I'm not sure if buckshot will.

"Ted?" she calls out in that sickly sweet voice of hers, which, if my emotions weren't supercharged on adrenaline, I could almost mistake for one of uxorious love. "Is that you, hon?"

I shudder with sick anticipation. My whole life's imploding. My job, lost. Savings gone. I'll never see my house, friends, loved ones again. In a week, I'll be dead and never see anything again. Perhaps stupidest of all, at the top of my mind, is the fact that I won't get to see who was under the ostrich mask in that stupid TV show. The next episode won't air for three more days.

That's life. That's my life. Over.

I open my mouth to reply, but they are whispering again. Annette pushes her key into the lock. Shit, shit, shit. Well, there's nothing for it. I discharge the shotgun.

Annette cries out in abbreviated pain.

"Mom!" Henry wails.

"Dammit, Ted!" Annette cries.

So the door offers pretty decent protection, but something hit her. I toss the shotgun down and grimacing in pain, struggle to pull the chaise lounge in front of the door.

"If you're infected, you need to turn yourself in. Do you know what'll happen to us if you . . . ah, goddammit!"

Annette moans in pain. She really must be hurt. Normally, she never takes the Lord's name in vain. Period. Let alone in front of the boy.

"I'm not infected!" I roar. God, this chaise is heavy. "I tried to tell the boy. I just fell and hurt myself. It just looks like an infection. But I swear it's not."

"He's lying, Mom," Henry says, "I saw it myself. We're going to get in trouble if we don't report it."

"This is why self-reporting is mandatory, Ted. So families don't have to go through this!"

I jam the chaise up into the doorknob. It won't hold for terribly long, but maybe long enough for me to figure something out. They're whispering again.

"There's nothing to report!" I shout back. "Nothing to report at all. Just an ordinary, no fuss, no muss wound."

I wipe my forehead. God, I'm sweating like a whore in church. I look to the back door. It's all glass. Not meant to be terrible secure. I've never really thought about that before. A thief could get in here and murder my entire family. I mean, assuming I don't finish the job myself right now.

" . . . around back."

Shit! I stumble forward. Henry's not exactly a sprinter. He's kind of a tubby little shit, actually. But he's still a kid and I'm over forty. And I never was much of a runner anyway, even before crippling myself earlier today.

Still, I've got to try for it. All I have to do is make it back to the glass door, down the porch, across the lawn and through the garden, then over the back fence before Henry can make it around the side.

Ah, shit. He's already there. Standing behind the glass. Grinning at me, that little shit. And he didn't come with just his dick in his hands this time, either. He's holding the hedge clippers, which, for safety's sake, I've never let him use before. Typical of his mother to undercut me. He snaps the clippers in the air twice threateningly, then points at my dick, the dick he squirted out of, that fuck! I can't level the shottie fast enough.

Literally. He turns and runs before I can get a bead on him. The front door is jingling, but the chaise seems to be holding for now. Annette, wounded, can't get the chaise unstuck. They think they can outflank me.

"Mother . . . little shit," I grumble.

That's all right. Henry's just a little kid. He's stupid. I know exactly what he's doing. I don't have to go back around front. I limp into the kitchen and lift the gun, pointing it through the side window. And there he goes, the pudgy little fuck, trampling through the side garden, knocking down all of his mother's carefully cultivated flowers, like we've told him not to a thousand times.

His head explodes into a geyser of blood and steel particles. My first clean, perfect shot of the day.

"Yes!" I cry, pumping my fist.

To add sprinkles to my victory sundae, he tumbles, fat belly forward, and torso plants right into the hedge clippers he'd been meaning to castrate me with. Serves you right, you little fucker.

"Henry!"

The makeshift barricade has finally failed and Annette is behind me, her cardigan riddled with tiny holes, and soaked red with blood. I can't remember what color it was when she left in the morning. I suppose she'll hold that against me too, just like when I can't remember what color her nails were or what haircut she had before the new one.

I point the shotgun at her. I have her dead to rights. I pull the trigger.

And, of course, I just killed the kid, so the damn thing isn't loaded. I fumble in my pocket and all of the cartridges tumble to the ground, because someone like me doesn't deserve to have good things happen to him.

"You killed our son, Ted," Annette says, advancing on me.

I grunt and groan in pain, trying to lower myself to the ground. "He was going to kill me first!"

Annette crosses her arms angrily. "That's the law, Ted. You're supposed to self-report. And when you don't . . . "

She reaches into the knife block and pulls out the biggest knife I've ever seen. I mean, seriously. I didn't even know we had this goddamned machete in our kitchen. I've certainly never seen her use it before. Women and their culinary secrets.

I fall over on my side, startled. The fall probably saves my life, because when the knife comes down, it buries deep into the flesh of my already wounded leg. Well, that's not ideal, but at least I'm not dealing with two wounded limbs now.

I kick at her with my good leg, and scrabble around on the floor, sending little red shotgun shells tumbling out of my pocket and scattering to the four corners of the kitchen, all dreadfully out of reach.

Annette scrabbles at me now, apparently trying to retrieve the kitchen cleaver from my leg for a second go at me. My leg is squirting blood. I guess she must have pierced an artery or something. That won't be good for very long. Do we have bandages or antiseptics down here? I know we keep some under the bathroom sink in the master bedroom, but I'm not sure what the hell Annette keeps under the kitchen sink.

Frustrated, I throw the gun in her direction like I was the villain in a goddamned "Superman" movie. She dodges, buying me a few precious seconds, and I practically yank the cabinet off its hinges. There are rolls of paper towels which should be good for blotting. But there's something else there too.

I twist the childproof seal off the gallon of bleach, ruminating briefly that Henry will never have the opportunity to do this to his own wife, or even learn how to break through a child seal, and splash bleach in Annette's eyes. Annette screams and recoils, so I keep splashing. She crab walks backwards across the linoleum, losing purchase as the bleach wets the floor. Finally, I toss the entire bottle in her direction and she dodges, as she did from the gun.

Bracing myself, I yank the knife out of my calf and press an entire roll of paper towels against my gaping new wound.

"Goddammit, Ted," Annette moans in blind agony. "All you had to do was self-report!"

"Oh, climb the fuck down off my back sometime." I swing the enormous knife blade into her forehead.

It takes me longer than it probably should, a solid thirty seconds maybe, as I lay there catching my breath, trying not to bleed out on the bleach-and-blood-covered kitchen floor before I realize I'm not alone. I look up.

Three-year-old Missy is standing in the kitchen doorway, thumb in mouth, teddy bear dangling from one hand.

"Dah-ddy?" she whispers, for all the world like Cindy Lou Who.

I sigh and crawl to my knees. "Come here, baby," I say, holding out my arms for a big paternal hug.

She shuffles nearer but stops, looking down at Annette's still twitching corpse. Actually, no, scratch that. Annette's not dead yet. She is staring up at us with a mixture of terror and condemnation, slowly choking to death on her own blood and a big old honking blade.

"What happened to Moh-mmy?" Missy asks, her voice curious but weirdly detached.

"Mommy had a little accident," I say, converting my hugging arms into one extended holding arm. Almost out of habit, Missy takes my hand. Kneeling, I'm pretty close to her eye level.

"Missy, honey, Daddy has a very important question to ask you."

"Okay, Daddy," she says, ever proud to be treated like a big girl.

"Now it's very important that you answer me truthfully. No fibbing like I know you do sometimes. Only the truth, you promise?"

"I pomise, Dah-ddy."

"You pinkie swear?"

She nods vehemently. I hold out my pinkie finger with the hand that is not clutching a rapidly soaking roll of paper towels to my leg. She takes my pinkie with her own, the most solemn of vows a three-year-old can make.

"Do you know about mandatory bite reporting?"

She nods, twice, hard. "Yes, Dah-ddy. Moh-mmy explained it to me a bunch of times, and we even watched the newsman explain it. I don't understand everything, but I understand that."

I nod. "Okay, good. It's very important that you know these things."

I take her head in my hands and swiftly snap her neck, eliciting a concerned burble from Annette, but that seems to have finally taken the last of the life out of her. Henry, Missy, and now, finally, taking her damn time to get ready as always, my wife, lay silent. I lower my daughter's still corpse to the ground.

Safe at last. Thank God. But what a mess to clean up! Nosy Mrs. Jenkins could be over any minute and spot Henry's body in the side garden. I'd love to at least take a break, but I really need to get all these corpses into the crawlspace or somewhere.

I glance down at my leg. My bandage is soaked with coagulated blood having turned a deep black, globs of yellow pus floating within.

"Oh, shit," I mutter.

I guess I was infected after all.

Stephen Kozeniewski (pronounced "causin' ooze key") is a two-time winner of the World Horror Grossout Contest. His published works have been nominated for several Splatterpunk, Voice Arts, and Indie Horror Book Awards, among other honors. He lives in Pennsylvania with his girlfriend and their two cats above a fanciful balloon studio.

# THE CHIROPRACTOR

## AARON THOMAS MILSTEAD

**I**'VE BEEN ARRESTED for statutory rape; spent a few stints in alcohol and drug rehab; been investigated by the FBI when I sent letters to Osama Bin Laden as part of an 'art project,' and I was threatened with incarceration when I was caught making a video of myself masturbating into a hole in the ground at a park in San Augustine—which, for the record, was a political statement.

I guess you could say I've got a few skeletons in my closet. All considering, it makes perfect sense that I decided to become a chiropractor. Of course, I managed to fuck that up too and I had to surrender my Texas license less than a year after I got it. I'd been running a decent operation out of my doublewide, but the real cash started coming in after I began treating particularly damaged patients with telepathy.

I told 'em I could go back in time and realign their bones and joints at the point they were damaged through an advanced technique which utilized telekinetic vibration. I called the process Pre-emergent Resonance, or Shadow Shifting, depending upon my mood and the IQ of the patient. For this treatment, I charged triple my usual rate: $90.00 an hour.

Obviously, it was total horseshit.

I copped insanity when I was busted, and the Texas Chiropractic regulators diagnosed me with 'delusional disorder.' The truth is, I was just a greedy son of a bitch. With my license barred and a potential stint in Huntsville should I continue practicing my craft, I was left with the prospect of shaving my balls and posing for the centerfold of "Man Overboard." I had a Bic razor hovering just above my taint when I heard a loud bang on my flimsy door. I wrapped a towel around my girthful unit and opening the door, I saw a redheaded man wearing a wife-beater and shorts so tight I could see his moose knuckle.

I'm six-foot four-inches and this asshole was taller than me. He had a glint in his eye, and my first thought was I'd probably fucked his wife. Or mother. So when he barged into my doublewide, uninvited, I almost dropped towel and sprinted for the closet where I kept my 45.

"Buford Pellerin," he said, extending a large hand that swallowed mine like a seasoned porn star. He squeezed it too hard and held it too long, and when I pulled away from him, he was smirking and his moose knuckle shifted. "I need your services." There was a perceptible menace in his deep southern voice that elicited a primal fear more extreme than a water moccasin slowly slithering by, an aversion akin to the thought of stepping barefoot into a steaming pile of dog shit.

Dismissing the part of my psyche that should have evolved long ago, I asked for clarification.

He grinned and said, "I'm willing to pay big."

He had my attention and, depending on his definition of *big,* I was willing to look past his overzealous handshake. I grabbed him a can of Natural Lite out of the fridge, and he sat down on the couch while I went into the back and dressed in my pink scrubs—so chosen because that color best showed off my spray-on tan.

Buford had already fetched a second can of Natty Lite out of the fridge and was watching Judge Judy on the tube when I came out of the back holding a bottle of massage oil. He smirked, looking me up and down as if he wanted to call me a fag. I was going to explain to him that pink was the new black when he asked, "You mind going to Lake Charles?"

The question caught me by surprise. I figured Buford wanted me to repair some bulging discs from the time he tried to tip a cow and it fell on him or when he damaged his lower back trying to blow himself. I was wrong. He wanted to secure my services for someone who resided smack dab in the anus of the universe—otherwise known as Louisiana. It was time to question what a coonass redhead in short shorts defined as "paying big."

I asked him.

"Five grand."

Apparently, our definitions weren't so far off. "Lake Charles sounds great."

We loaded into a brown ford sporting a massive cattle guard and a bumper sticker that read: NOBODY LISTENS TO ME TILL I FART. As we sped down a bumpy dirt road, I asked, "Who do you need me to work on?"

Buford stared ahead as he navigated the narrow dirt road and said, "Paw Paw Diggs. He's my grandpa."

"What happened to him?"

"He got in a wreck and was tossed through the windshield. Broke his neck."

"I see."

I was getting a bad feeling. It was easy enough to convince a hypochondriac that Shadow Shifting was beneficial, but if some old fart had been reduced to vegetable status, it was going to be impossible to fake. Of course, at five grand a pop, I might be able to convince them it would take several treatments to reverse such severe trauma. Before the final treatment, I'd be somewhere beyond the Mexican border enjoying prostitutes and Tequila Sunrises, and every time short shorts changed out the old man's colostomy bag, he could think of me.

"Is that a problem?" Buford asked.

"Not at all," I said, smiling. "Every bit as common as a bulging disc. Child's play for someone of my considerable skills."

Buford nodded solemnly. "Good."

As if determined to fulfill the most blatant of stereotypes, Buford popped in a mix tape comprised of zydeco songs and pre-'60s country. He hummed along while I mentally constructed earmuffs, blinders, and slipped on a body condom and then climbed into a protective bubble like the one John Travolta lived in when he played the sick kid in that made-for-TV movie. I carefully considered how many five-thousand-dollar treatments I could squeeze out of the saps before starting my new life as a Mexican.

About an hour later, I shivered as we passed over an invisible barrier and went from Texas to Louisiana. In my mind's ear I could hear that old Cajun screaming, "I gayruntee!"

The pine trees dried out and the paved roads began to deteriorate, and a toxic fart bubble seemed to descend upon the dreary landscape. I suddenly felt fully justified in referring to blacks as "colored" and wondered if I'd ever accidentally fucked my sister.

Entering Louisiana requires a mind shift.

We drove through Lake Charles and moved down a network of dirt roads that grew bumpier, narrower, jarring my bones and sending up red clouds behind us. Buford never slowed down.

We snaked deeper and further away from civilization, and I began to wonder if I was being taken to some sort of cannibalistic, hillbilly shin dig where I was going to be the main course with a side order of etouffee. I wished I'd tucked my 45 into my front pocket.

The sun was setting when we pulled up to a shithole of a house covered with Christmas lights and siding that had turned green with mold. George Strait was droning on in his ridiculous mock twang about "Ocean Front Property" as Buford killed the truck.

A screen door flung open, and a kid ran toward the truck. Buford snatched him up and swung him into the air. The kid kind of looked happy while he gurgled, though it might have been laughter. I'm not exactly sure what the politically correct term is for this (I've heard 'special' thrown around a bit), but the kid had issues. For one thing, he seemed to be about four or five years old, but he was still wearing a diaper and judging from the brown avocado juice running down the kid's leg he had shit himself. Also, the kid's eyes seemed to be too far apart and he had a ridiculous smile permanently plastered on his face, even though it was perfectly clear there wasn't a goddamned thing to be happy about. I'll add that the kid was literally covered with mosquito bites, so child protective services should probably have gotten involved, but that's discounting the fact that in Louisiana there are no social services. Even if there were, that kid was already considered legally old enough to smoke, drink, and marry his cousin.

Next person to come out and greet us was Buford's wife. You probably are like me and you already had her pegged as the typical Louisiana swamp trash—mouth filled with yellowed Chiclets, greasy hair, and leathery skin roughened from a lifetime of hard work and Menthols. Boy, was I wrong. She was a short little blonde, at least ten years younger than Buford, with a pair of knockers that would make Dolly Parton envious. She looked a lot like Suzanne Somers during the Three's Company years—back before she made that shitty sitcom with the guy from Dallas and tried to sell Thighmasters.

This hot piece of ass ran up to Buford and stuck her tongue so far down his throat that Short Shorts gagged. So did I. I'm going to be describing some things that make the *X-Files* look like an episode of *The Real World*, but that marriage remains the most mysterious thing I've ever seen.

Buford introduced us, and the wife told me the kid was named John McLane, after the Bruce Willis character in the *Die Hard* movies. I figured she was setting the bar a little high, considering the kid was in the process of digging into his diaper and making mud pies. On the other hand, I don't guess it's fair to name every 'special needs' kid Corky.

We stepped into a living room that looked like it had been designed by Martha Stewart's white trash cousin—patchwork blankets tacked to the walls and a lime green couch covered with plastic. There was a cabinet filled with a collection of glass and porcelain dairy cows. Their TV had rabbit ears. The place smelled of cornbread and welfare. The thought of those yokels pulling together five grand was beyond far-fetched and I quit collecting porcelain figurines back in the early '80s.

Buford watched me surveying the digs, and though I wouldn't have pegged him as the perceptive type, he said, "There's a gas well on Paw Paw's property that hit about six years ago and makes about four grand a month."

"Fair enough." I resisted the urge to make a Beverly Hillbillies reference, though as I think back on it the hot blonde might have been named Ellie May.

"Maw Maw is resting in the back," Buford said. "Before we wake her up, I need to make a few things clear. She's still as sharp as a whip, but she's pretty old."

"Yeah?"

"Yeah. She's ninety-four. Also . . . she's Malagasy."

"What's that?" I asked.

He told me she was born in Madagascar and what's more, that she's black. In fact, good old pale red-headed Buford's coonass was one-fourth black himself. Over seventy years ago, Paw Paw rescued her from a life of poverty in Madagascar and drug her clear across the world to America in order to enjoy a life of poverty. If you find Madagascar on a globe and put your finger directly on the other side, then you will hit Louisiana. I didn't know squat about Madagascar or their unique customs, but I was damn sure about to find out.

Buford led me into a bedroom and introduced me to a little brown lump that was buried beneath an ocean of blankets. She opened her eyes and asked me, "You the Shadow Shifter?" Her voice was damn near as deep as James Earl Jones.

"Yeah." I tried to remember all the saps I had sold that bill of good; nothing like word-of-mouth advertisement to drum up business. "How'd you hear about me?"

"I told Maw Maw about you," Buford said. "Last year, I worked on a rig with a fella named Bryant Cook. We called him Tea Bag. He told us you treated his wife, and she went from barely being able to turn her neck to full recovery."

"Dee Dee Cook," I said. "I remember her. She was a mess, but I straightened her out. She told me she got thrown from a horse."

"Tea Bag told us he got drunk and smacked her around a little too hard. Whichever it was, you earned your money. He said she was like a new woman. That you fixed the damage like it never happened. Breathed new life into her."

"That's what I do," I lied. Truth is, Dee Dee was healthy as a horse and *treatment* consisted of a five-minute neck rub and fifty-five minutes of rough sex. I didn't do a damn thing to repair her alleged injury, but I certainly improved her flexibility. I'd have to come up with a different treatment strategy for Paw Paw's injury, but I still planned on screwing them out of as much of that gas-well money as possible. "Where's Paw Paw?"

"He's waiting on us," Maw Maw said, her tiny pink tongue flashing out from between stacks of dark wrinkles.

"Where?" I asked.

"Out back." Buford opened the closet door and pulled out a shotgun and aimed it in the general direction of my genitals.

71

# THE CHIROPRACTOR

Retarded Die Hard stumbled into the room and shouted, "Da Da" and threw a handful of shit at me. It was shaping up to be a rough day.

I remained very still while Ellie May helped Maw Maw out of the bed and eased her over to a walker. John McLane kept calling me "Da Da" and played with his feces like it was Playdoh, smearing it on the wall and occasionally tossing it at me. No one else seemed to notice.

I asked Buford why he felt the need to pull a shotgun on me and he explained that he figured Tea Bag was a moron and wrong about my abilities. Buford had felt the need to tell Maw Maw about me in the event that I was a genuine "faith healing-shadow-shifting-extraordinaire," but if I wasn't, then that was fine too. He'd just blow my fucking head off.

Maw Maw interjected that I had "kind eyes and a trustworthy face."

The five of us went out into the backyard and slowly moved down a trail that led into the woods behind their house. I was escorted between Buford and Bruce Willis Jr. Maw Maw crept behind me with a rocker that had tennis balls planted on the tips. She was like a little wrinkled shadow behind us with a deep, intimidating voice—bizarro world's version of Mike Tyson. Like any other old broad, she couldn't get enough of her own voice and she prattled on about the old days when she was a little girl in Madagascar. Some of what she said was damn near indecipherable because she would float between English and French. From best I could tell, either she had been a slave or her parents were. Apparently, there was some kind of caste system and the darker the skin, the lower you ranked. That put Maw Maw at the bottom of the food chain, and too bad Buford hadn't been around back then because judging from his pasty ass, he would have been the king of the country.

She said it was a beautiful land. Rice paddies were laid out like the squares in a quilt and the red mountains were covered with pine trees. In spots, the rivers ran from the mountains into the ocean and it looked like Madagascar was bleeding. She said that the people there were very poor and lived in shacks, but they saved up all of their lives for one thing: a family tomb. Apparently, the central Malagasy belief is that death is more important than life—that dead ancestors are considered to be potent forces that the family continues to share time with.

She said something I couldn't exactly understand, but she repeated it, and then Buford growled at me and repeated it as well—the turning of the bone. The process sounded a bit like a description of chiropractory, but a few minutes later the path ended, and the truth settled in on me like an itch that precedes crabs or the clap.

I'd either been marched out to the Lake Charles' county fair or the Pellerin family cemetery. Maybe both. An old iron gate as orderly and inviting as rusted barbed wire surrounded an area that was at least a few acres. Gaudy Christmas lights had been strung around the top of the fence and ran in an endless flashing procession of green, red, blue, yellow, and orange. Plastic pink flamingos, pinwheels, garden gnomes, and bird feeders mingled amidst the headstones or freestanding concrete tombs. Picnic tables with green umbrellas were situated at each of the four inside corners.

Inside the gate, the orderly rows of headstones were occasionally broken by somber statues of angels. Buford stepped up and took out a key ring and unlocked a thick chain and swung open the gate.

I took a deep breath and asked, "Is Paw Paw in there?"

"Of course he is," Buford said.

For once, I was at a loss for words. I've seen and done some crazy shit, but I'd finally flown over the cuckoo's nest and landed inside, and the big Indian chucked the oversized paperweight to get us out, but it landed on my head instead.

I was fucked.

Night had settled around us and the fog was rising. Frogs sung ambiguous songs that I imagine were at least as articulate as Lady GaGa. Buford reminded me that he was holding a shotgun by tapping me on the forehead with its muzzle and gestured for me to walk into the cemetery.

I stepped in and immediately noticed a headstone shaped like a penis with the name Dewey Delacroix etched into it. I walked past several Delacroixs and some Thibadeauxs, Savois, a handful of Boudreauxs and then an ocean of Pellerins—which seemed to be getting the preferential treatment because several of them were adorned with fresh flowers.

The ground in front of two of the headstones was soft. Daniel Wortham Pellerin and Christine Anne Smith-Pellerin. "That's my folks," Buford said.

I nodded.

Daniel had died almost fifteen years before and Christine over eight years. The ground in front of them was soft.

Buford gestured at one of those free-standing concrete tombs—it was smack dab in the middle of the Pellerin headstones. Paw Paw was waiting for me in there?

Ellie May yelled, "Johnny!" and I looked up and saw Bruce Willis Jr. had stripped off his diaper and was running circles around a statue of an angel that seemed on the verge of weeping. Poor little bastard had a penis the size of a Flintstone vitamin. Maw Maw inched past me and disappeared inside the concrete tomb. A moment later, it began to glow inside and a moment after that, music poured out. It was Ronnie Milsap singing, "There Ain't No Getting Over Me."

I glanced over at Buford and asked, "What are you expecting of me?"

"Not a damned thing," he said. "But Maw Maw is expecting a lot."

"And if Maw Maw is disappointed?"

"Then you get buried next to the Delacroixs. They're just distant kin anyway."

"I see."

Buford pressed the muzzle of the gun into my kidney and pushed me toward the mouth of the tomb. I ducked and stepped into a space just a bit larger than the bathroom in my single-wide. A Coleman battery operated lantern hung from the ceiling. A boom box and dozens of potted plants lined the concrete shelves. Maw Maw was rocking to the gentle rhythms of Ronnie Milsap—the blind master of the feathered mullet. A plastic sheet covered a bundle that was stretched out in front of her on a concrete slab.

Maw Maw looked up at me and said, "Bring him back to me."

The air reeked like Menudo gone bad and I stared at the sheet. "How long has he been gone?"

"Eighty-two days." Buford stepped into the space behind me. The shotgun hovered about three inches from my family jewels. A second later, Ellie May and Die Hard Jr. squeezed into the tight, murky space. Dolly Parton and Kenny Rogers were singing "Islands In the Stream." Maw Maw unrolled a section of sheet, and a nose and pale lips poked out. She leaned down and kissed the dead man.

Paw Paw.

My patient.

The smell of menudo grew stronger and now hinted of cheese. Maw Maw unrolled the rest of the sheet. Paw Paw was naked. His eyelids were held shut with twin sheets of black electrical tape. His lips had begun to peel back and there was a perfect set of too-white dentures shoved into his mouth. Cotton-balls were shoved into his ears. I glanced down and shuddered—there was a condom hanging from his saggy, flaccid penis and some sort of fluids had collected within its reservoir tip.

"To keep him from leaking, you got to cover up all the holes," Buford said defensively.

"Bring him back to me," Maw Maw repeated.

"But he's dead," I mumbled.

"You're the shadow-shifter," Buford said. "Best shift back before he got into that car wreck and repair his broken neck."

"He's old," I said. "How do you know it was even the broken neck that killed him?"

"I know," Buford said. "I was driving the car."

I shuffled over next to Maw Maw and considered my options. I could try to take the shotgun away from Buford, but chances were he'd shoot off my junk first. I could refuse to treat Paw Paw, but chances were, Buford would yet again kill my sex life. I figured the best bet was to fake like I was

Jesus fucking Christ and pretend to resurrect the smelly, wrinkled bag of foul menudo and tell them I was making progress but it would take time. See you next week. Then I'd take the five large and relocate my single-wide. It was a plan.

I stood over Paw Paw and finally allowed myself a careful look. It wasn't pretty. I didn't have to ask if they'd embalmed the body. In fact, I wasn't sure they'd even washed it. The skin looked loose and though he was mostly bald, there were patches of gray hair growing like cobwebs. His midsection looked mildly pregnant, but the rest of him was bulimic and weak. Dark liver spots covered his pale face and stood out like his pepperoni shaped nipples.

All eyes were on me, waiting for me to touch him. Kenny Rogers chanted: "Islands in a stream. That is what we are. Nothing in between. How can we be wrong?"

My hands hovered over his cantaloupe shaped head. His nose seemed to have continued growing even after his heart stopped. Bloated belly filled with Menudo; brazen penis resting atop a wrinkled mound of dead sperm. I had an epiphany that maybe being a con-artist was the wrong path. When I was a child, I was convinced I'd grow up to be a zookeeper, and I'd spend my time teaching sign language to gorillas and nursing albino tigers with a baby bottle.

I reached down and put my hands on Paw Paw's neck and the skin moved like a stewed tomato. I gently moved the head to the left and noticed mold growing on the back of his neck—soft green tendrils feeding on the decomposing flesh.

I jerked back and bumped into the nuzzle of the shotgun.

I leaned down towards Paw Paw and saw there was lipstick smudged on his curled lips and blotted on those perfect teeth. I reached down again and touched him as lightly as possible on either side of his neck. My fingers seemed to sink into his flesh and touch in the middle.

There was an invisible hum like countless flies, and I was aware of my own heartbeat. I could feel it in my temples and rising beneath my chest.

"Bring him back to me," Maw Maw begged from a distant somewhere.

Thoughts flashed through my mind. This isn't right. There's nothing left of him. If he had been alive, I'd have told him to remember the moment of the accident. What it was like the instant of the wreck. That feeling of helplessness. The impact and the moment of trauma. Then I'd ask him to think about the moments before. The feeling of being in the car and whole and untouched by the moment to come.

I'd make him fixate on that.

Then I'd wiggle his head around and tell him I'd taken some of it away. Eventually, I'd tell him I'd taken it all away.

This was different. There was nothing left to take away.

I was thinking about that and trying to ignore the phantom hum and I could see death in front of me and feel it behind me. The skin beneath my fingers was sliding away and lower, was just bone and menudo. I was about to tell Buford that it was going to take more time when Paw Paw's eyelids flew open and the strips of black tape peeled away. His eyeballs had sunk down somewhere into the darkness of his head.

"Jesus Christ," Buford said.

Paw Paw's dentures parted, and a scream erupted from his mouth.

I pulled away from him—my fingers left dents in the sides of his thin neck.

The corpse screamed like a newborn—fearful and unsure.

Maw Maw took Paw Paw's head in her hands and cradled it. Paw Paw screamed and his hands tore at the saggy skin of his chest and dug in—tore away a nipple and sunk down to the bone. The flesh was soft as Jello and the menudo leaked out of him.

"Grab his arms," Buford screamed and Ellie May jumped in and grabbed his right one, but Paw Paw dug into his bloated stomach with his left and glistening black entrails spilled out.

Buford jumped in and held his left arm down and all the while Maw Maw kept kissing his face. His screams only got louder.

Little Willis Jr. cried.

I pushed past them all and stumbled out of the tomb.

Still the dead man screamed.

Inside the tomb, the shotgun roared.

The clouds opened, and it began to drizzle.

As I ran away, the shotgun roared four more times behind me.

Aaron T. Milstead lives in the Piney Woods of East Texas with his wife and three children. He is a Lecturer at Stephen. F. Austin University and is the author of the horror novel *They Don't Check Out* and *Ear Worm* published through Blood Bound Books. He was also featured in *Road Kill Vol 3* and *Crash Code*. Other publications include the short stories "Identical, Only Different", "A Succession of Nearly Identical Ripples", "The Pickled Man", "Castration Complex", "Ways the World Breaks You Down", "Rampant Immorality"; "A Losing Battle" and "Take Your Time".

# PDF

## Lucas Milliron

"YOU'RE TURNING INTO your phone, dude," Ethan said before biting a fork full of salad.

"Man, you've got no idea what the hell is going on out there!" Jacob said, fingers sliding across the screen his eyes were glued to.

"Um." Ethan looked out the window. "Raining?"

"No!" Jacob slammed the phone on the table. "Have you seen what's going on with the trains derailing? Or that the government FINALLY admitted Covid came from a lab?"

"Seriously man." Ethan put both his elbows on the table and rested his forehead on his cold fists. "It's one rabbit hole after another. If it's not Musk buying Twitter or Bill Gates buying farmland, it's a fucking meme!"

"Because you won't look for yourself!"

"I watch the news."

"Oh, that corporate curated propaganda machine?"

"Yeah, I know it's biased. But I don't have time to fall down these weird conspiracy traps."

"I guess I just can't live my life woefully ignorant."

"It's not about being ignorant. That shit's too stressful. I got offline because I had a fucking heart attack last month! I'm only thirty-five!"

"Dad died of a heart attack. It kinda runs in the family."

"Yeah, a heart attack at seventy-eight! I'm just telling you; I've been down that path before. You can't carry the world's problems. You can only tend the garden you can reach."

Jacob held up his phone. "World Wide Web at my fingertips. Guess I can reach a lot farther than you think."

"Remember when we were kids, and we used to stay up all night playing that video game Duke Nukem?"

"The reboot was shit."

"Fucking garbage!" He agreed with his brother. "Dude, I found an old

N64 *AND* a copy of Duke Nukem 3D online! Jen's got the kids for the weekend; it'll be like old times."

"Old times sucked."

"It's moms birthday. Can we at least pretend to be brothers again?"

"I don't want to relive the old times."

"Fine. I tried. Dad was right."

"Hey!" Jacob stopped scrolling to look up from his text. "Don't be shitty."

"I'm being shitty? I've barely seen your face this entire meal! I bet you don't even know what restaurant we're in without googling it!"

"We're in," Jacob stopped and looked around. "Olive Garden."

"Fucking Carrabba's! You've been looking at your phone since you sat in my car! You're obsessed. This isn't healthy."

Jacob dropped his head and kept his eye on the phone.

"We can't all be perfect like you," he said.

"Fuck you." Ethan said.

Jacob regretted it the moment he said it but didn't do anything to correct it. No apologies, no explanations, only silence until the waitress came back with the check.

Ethan pulled out his card and paid for dinner, then rolled his wheelchair out of the restaurant's narrow walkways. Jacob was right behind, face glued to his phone. His thumbs slid across the glass like warm ice. He tapped images and touched links, burying himself in the rest of the world's problems.

Deeper, Jacob dug himself in Substack articles about Russian Troll farms controlling the top 20 most popular Christian Facebook Groups. Another article, this on the World Economic Forum, stating, "You will own nothing and you will be happy." The guest lists as scandalous and evasive as Epstein's guest book.

There was a documentary on cobalt mining, with images of emaciated women in the Congo mining the toxic mineral bare handed, their babies wrapped and tied to their bodies. The minerals that powered the globe electric motor found in every lithium battery from iPhone, to Tesla's, to hearing aids, all from the broken backs of modern African slaves.

Jacob looked up from his phone and out the window. Rain drops tapped the glass, popping with colors of amber headlights and red and green stoplights. He looked at the black face of his cell phone as the screen turned off and saw his reflection staring back like some black mirror. His face was gaunt, his clothes baggy. He'd hardly eaten since their mother passed away eight months ago.

The thought of her sent his mind in a downward spiral of anxiety. Jacob's nerve endings lit up across his back like jellyfish under his skin.

He grabbed his stomach as it twisted in knots. Burps and bile crept up the back of his throat in a sour tasting slurry.

Mom would probably say, sip some 7-Up for his stomach and rub Vicks VapoRub on his feet for the pain. It didn't always work, but that wasn't the point. Mom always had an answer. Tears welled in the corner of his eyes, stinging as he tried not to hold it all in. Mom was gone. His brother was broken. He was a fuck-up.

Jacob's fingers were unlocking his phone before he'd even noticed. Any escape would be better than this. Despite the landmines of social justice warriors and QAnon nut bags, the online world was a safe escape from his miserable life. Watching train derailments and covid wards was like watching animals at a zoo, safely behind glass. His neck ached from craning to look down at his phone while his hands and fingers cramped holding it, but the reels, videos and memes kept coming. Anything for a cheap hit of serotonin.

They rode in silence, Eathan behind the wheel. His Suburban SUV was outfitted for disabled drivers. He drove with one hand on the wheel, and the other on a joystick that worked the foot pedals.

Jacob scrolled to a reel of a man skydiving. He pulled his parachute, but the line was tangled. He cut it free and pulled his axillary to the same effect. Jacob watched safely in his brother's car as the man's body bounced once on impact, then settled into the dirt with a heavy thud.

An ad popped up on his screen so large it covered most of the website. It was something stupid about seeing worlds beyond limitation. Jacob tried to click the X and close the window, but the button moved. He tried again, but like a stubborn fly, the X moved away from his finger.

The SUV took a heavy bump and Jacob flinched, looking up from his phone. He blinked away its bright blue glow, trying to get his eyes to normalize in the evening gloom. Ethan was still driving, still focused on the road and not saying a thing. Jacob looked back at his phone. His thumb must have hit the link instead of the X, because his phone was downloading a file. When it finished, the file opened a video and began to play. Jacob's eyes widened at what he saw.

It was their father's retirement party, filmed and edited like some amateur documentarian. It was held as the Polish Club off Lake Worth road. Ethan was drunk on the dance floor before Jacob even arrived.

"This is your fault, you know," their father had said to Jacob. "Your brother's drunk because *HE* delt with the food trucks by himself! Why don't you help? Oh, cause you're a deadbeat. You could have been so much better than that, but you couldn't even finish school."

"*Mi amor*, please!" their mother said, her voice on the verge of tears. "Don't do this now. People are watching."

"Let them watch!" he said. "I already told them our sons are worthless. They know. They have eyes. I have no pity for these kids.

"Jacob, *mijo*," their mother asked, "where's your brother?"

"I don't know." Jacob rolled his eyes. "Wasn't my turn to babysit."

"Ethan left!" Jen said, her face flush with anger. "Left all of us!"

"He can't drive!" their mother said, "he's been drinking! *Mijo*! Jacob, we need to go find him!"

Jacob sighed. The only upside was at least he'd escape the stupid party. They rushed out, hopped into their mother's car, and left.

The scene faded to black as they stepped outside, then faded back to Ethan's Tesla wrapped around a tree near a ditch in a dark, wooded road. The front end of the car, from the hood to the steering wheel, was crushed into a brick of twisted metal. Ethan opened the door and tried to get out but couldn't move. The dashboard and steering wheel pinned him to his seat. He grabbed the oh-shit bar above the door and pulled.

Tears dripped onto the screen and obscured the images on Jacob's phone as he watched his brother's bloodied body emerge from the wreckage. Jacob felt his heart beating in his throat when he heard a tearing sound like wet denim. A red stain-soaked Ethan's pants and shirt. He grunted as he pulled with all his might. With a wet, meaty rip, Ethan tore himself out of the driver's seat and collapsed in the dirt.

Seconds later, Jacob and their mother pulled up to the scene. They parked Mom's car as Ethan dragged himself away from the wreckage. A trail of glistening red traced his path, while dirt and pine needles stuck to his wet face and chest. Their mother, who was a nurse when she was younger, rushed to Ethan's side.

"Take off his belt!" she said. "Yours too!"

Jacob did as he was told and handed them to his mother. She tied the tourniquet around the top of his thighs, close to his pelvis. She held Ethan down while Jacob tightened the knots. Ethan screamed.

Jacob remembered his brother's blood slick between his fingers. He looked at the carnage below his brother's waist. Strips of meat clung to ribbons of skin like torn jeans where his legs used to be. His pants were shredded and soaked with crimson.

"We need to call for help!" their mother said.

Jacob pulled out his phone, but with so much blood caked on his fingers, even the phone wanted nothing to do with all the gore. His face flushed with tears, Jacob wiped his brother's blood on his shirt and unlocked his phone. As he called for help, the video finished playing.

Back in Ethan's new car, Jacob cleared his throat and patted the corners of his eyes dry. He didn't look up from the phone, who's screen had gone black with the videos completion. His brother couldn't see him like this. Ethan lost more than his legs in the accident that night. Five years of recovery, both physical and substance abuse. His only reprieve was that no one else was hurt. He'd lost his wife in the divorce that followed and was forced to sell his food truck franchise to cover medical bills.

Now, not two years after their father died—neither brother mourned his passing—their mother finally succumbed to emphysema. You don't see pink-ribbon charity walks for lung cancer the way you do for breast cancer or heart disease. Because you were the one who chose to smoke cigarettes.

Life was just one damn thing after another.

A world of artificial starlight surrounded them on the journey from Carrabba's as they drove down Congress Ave in Boynton Beach. The strip malls and condominiums were bright amber specs against the windows as the rain began again. They were headed to Ethan's place where Jacob left his car.

Jacob felt useless. He couldn't do anything to save their mother. Ethan was too independent now to let anyone help him, let alone his college drop-out brother. School was pointless when the jobs you studied wouldn't pay back the loan it took to get them. Besides, most of the stuff they taught you, he could learn just as well in a few YouTube videos.

And that made Jacob the black sheep. The fuck-up with nothing to lose because he didn't have anything in the first place. He saw what success did to his brother. The constant stress of owning a business while balancing out a wife with kids on the spectrum. Life took its sacrifice, mostly through blood and sanity.

Jacob's palm buzzed as he received a notification link. He looked down and slid his thumb across the screen to unlock it, then flinched as a sharp pain shot through his digit. There was a small papercut on the tip, oozing a little blood. A single drop fell from his finger and landed on the screen over the strange link.

Too focused on his finger, he didn't notice the small crack in the screen healing as it absorbed his blood. By the time Jacob looked around for what he'd cut himself on, his phone was back to normal as it lit up as it began to download something else.

*Shit*, he thought.

Ethan parked the car, oblivious to his brother's injury.

Jacob went through his apps and tried to stop the download, but by the time he'd gotten to the home screen, the file was loaded. A PDF opened automatically. Before he could read it, Ethan closed the trunk and was wheeling himself around the car.

Jacob took a long breath through his nose and got out. Standing up, he felt a pull in his bladder.

"Need to take a leak," he said to Ethan, "then I'll head out."

# PDF

"Sounds good," Ethan said, opening the front door.

Jacob following his brother inside. He wasn't ready for another lecture, so he made a beeline straight for the bathroom. The guest water closet was a small room with just a toilet and sink. The walls were textured with geometric tiles whose angles and shapes protruded for a weird 3D effect. Jacob couldn't look at it for more than a second or two without getting a headache, so after dropping trou and sitting on the throne, he went back to his phone.

The PDF was an untitled document with around thirty-seven pages, still blank. He gave it a moment to load, watching as grey and red pixels peppered the screen like Lego bricks. They came together before his eyes, giving vague hints at the weird images beneath. It was some kind of eBook, the cover page was plain text reading, The Grimoires Speculum.

The pages that followed were a mix of strange optical illusions. Weird colors and chaotic designs dominated the pages, forcing the eyes to never stop scanning. The bathroom lights dimmed, and the screen cast a muddy red glow across Jacob's face.

Jacob's eyes scanned the slurry of colors and dots. It was like studying astrology without a star map. He found himself tracing imaginary lines, giving shapes to the random clusters of colorful pixels. Piece by piece, he caught glimpses of weird creatures hidden amongst the chaos of geometry. Silhouettes of faces wrecked with hideous torment. Emaciated figures, their limbs shimmering with prismatic colors.

So enthralled, Jacob didn't hear Ethan calling from behind the door. All sounds outside the bathroom were muffled as if heard underwater. The light of the screen grew brighter, the phone hot in his fingers, but his eyes kept dancing, tracing more lines, finding fresh details in the chaos of multicolored inkblots.

Everything came to a halt and his eyes crossed, producing a three-dimensional prize at the end of the puzzle. A sphere spun on an oblique axis in the middle of his screen. It was the color of rainbow and coal. Its edges darker than black, its shine brilliant as the cosmos. Weirder still, it looked as if he could just reach out and pluck it.

*But that's impossible*, he thought. *So why is my finger reaching for it?*

Jacob's hand was acting on its own accord. His finger touched the glass. The screen rippled as if he'd touched a still pond. The spinning sphere within radiated heat like a hot afternoon. Curiosity peaked, he reached inside and grabbed the sphere.

Ethan broke the door open with a broom handle. It was as if someone released an exterior hatch on a space station. A hellish wind blew from the bathroom, sucking everything not attached to the walls and floor into the house. The broom handle flew across the room as the door was torn from its hinges. Ethan grabbed the door frame with one hand, wheelchair in the other, struggling not to be blown away.

The sphere felt like touching a hot stove and Jacob withdrew his hand from the glass. Despite the pain, his other hand would not release the phone. Jacob grabbed it with his burnt hand to yank it from his grasp, but upon contact, his fingers became useless.

Ethan watched as the liquid glass melted away from the cellphone and washed up his brother's hand. It crackled like broken crystals and slithered under his skin through the nail beds. Jacob cried out as thousands of microscopic shards burrowed into his muscles, scraping his bones. The phone's battery glowed cherry red, its heat fusing the plastic to Jacob's smoldering fingers.

Behind the glass was blackness. A void so dark, even light couldn't escape its gravity. Two hands with six fingers, no thumbs, reached out of the phone and grabbed Jacob's wrists. Their pale digits were long and slender, the knuckles blue and fingers tips-stained pink.

A face emerged. Two black eyes of an abyssal fish glared from the top of a flat, amphibian head. Its thin lips peeled to show trillions of tiny, hooked teeth jetting out of blackened gums. Its pallid flesh was devoid of all color, save the purple and green veins stitched beneath its skin.

It slithered out of the screen, its flesh more a virtuous fluid than solid matter. The body of the creature was that of a soft bodied mantis, with long limbs and sharp barbs jutting from forearms and slender calves. Its slick skin glistened like oil over water. A stink of rotted fish and excrement filled the room as Jacob's bowels released their contents into the toilet.

The monstrosity released Jacob's hands and climbed out of the phone. Its size filled the space floor to ceiling and it squatted to better fit. Jacob's face bled as a thousand glass shards cut intricate sigils and strange geometries from beneath his skin. No longer in control of his own body, he stood up from the seat, his flaccid penis receding in an act of self-preservation.

The creature pressed its cold, slick hands against Jacob's face, tracing the glyphs, muttering in strange and inhuman tongues the words they read. It dug its nails into the top of Jacob's forehead at the hairline and began to peel off his face. Jacob's last act of willpower was a throat tearing scream of pain as the creature degloved skin from the meat.

Weaponless, Ethan threw himself onto the creature's back. He screeched in pain as long barbs sprouted from its back and skewered Ethan like a porcupine. Ethan cried out and he let himself fall to the floor. His body was a pincushion of quills. Venom from the barbs seeped into his bloodstream, firing off nerve endings in a lightning storm of pain throughout his body. His muscles spasmed as he curled into a ball, hot tears racing down his cheeks.

Jacob's face was draped over the creature's arm like a hand towel. The red meat beneath shimmered as blood poured down his neck, soaking into his green shirt. The glass under his skin sparkled like star dust between the delicate musculature. The creature spoke, but not through its mouth. Its words were a whisper, a faint echo of vowels singing to his subconscious.

*False face hides what false heart doth know. No more mask.*

"Who are you?" Jacob asked, his voice horse.

*I am the Curator. The one who shows what you want to see. You hide behind your skin, shielded by your glass and metal box. But its light carries no warmth. You seek catastrophe, vicarious, to mask the pain of your own apocalypse.*

Jacob said nothing, for he knew it to be true. His heart was racing, hands clammy. Reality was caving in around him, crushed by the gravity of his own depression. His mind scrolled through reels of hawks pecking meat off a cat's bones, a man stepping off the rail in front of a moving train. It's not voyeurism when you are the devoured.

*The universe is a mirror of our own consciousness. I will show you beyond the stars. Beyond this plane of suffering.*

Jacob watched his brother on the floor, writhing in pain. He remembered the accident, the way his brother crawled out of the wreckage, a snail's trail of gore behind him. His nubs still kicking, for his brain was unaware of the missing appendages.

He looked up at the creature, his mouth quivering in pain, and said, "Don't let my brother suffer."

*This I can promise.*

Jacob watched as his brother's convulsing eased. Ethan's sobs softened, though he stayed tightly curled in the fetal position. Jacob looked out the bathroom door into the house. Perhaps the lights were off or were swallowed by whatever void carried the creature to him.

The phone, still in Jacob's hand, began to vibrate. A bell rang from the void inside its screen.

*Come. It tolls for us.*

Faceless, Jacob took the creature's hand and followed him into oblivion.

# LUCAS MILLIRON

Lucas Milliron is a born and raised native Floridian, oldest of three siblings to a loving mother and father. Married to his wife, he still resides in South Florida as a Licensed eye care professional. Lucas Milliron, Weird Florida Fiction.

# PARTS

## ARLO GOREVIN

**K**NOW THIS. There is poetry in the dead. I might be standing in a cellar where the cobwebs sparkle with fresh red, or a bedroom of bare floorboards and moth-tattered curtains and sometimes I'll hear it, the voice of the Universe in eyes washed clean of their souls, a verse in offal already beginning to be honeycombed by an intimacy of flies. I've seen men blanch at such carnage, ashamed that their strong stomachs are lined with less steel than they claimed while I, a mere woman in their eyes, finds a poetry that endures. Death holds no abhorrence for me, and nor should it, for I myself was born of the grave.

Today I heard the verse standing in a bathroom of cracked tiles and bloody chrome with Traxler at my side.

"I know this man," I told Traxler, surveying the rag doll cadaver sprawled in its ungainly tangle upon the bathroom floor. 'I've seen him in your company. He was your friend?'"

I heard the leather of Traxler's jacket creak softly as he shrugged. "Business associate, and yeah, maybe you've seen him around the club a few times. All I know is that a couple of the boys were meant to put the frighteners on him, he got lippy, and well . . . things got a bit disorderly, as you can see."

*Disorderly.* The man's bald cranium had been cleaved from dome to brow, his blue eyes staring starkly at opposite walls. One of them seemed to have become unmoored, flooded and bloating in its socket. His brain was visible through the lips of riven skull, mushroom-pale as its blood settled into the lowest channels, a tangle of tissue like the wrinkled scalp of a Sphynx cat. One of his hands had been crushed, the splintered fingers drawn inward like the limbs of an expired spider. Whatever instrument sundered the wet valley in his head, be it an axe or machete, had been removed. *Good*, I thought. The elusive Mr. Dillon employed me to dispose of corpses, not weapons.

"So you can take care of it, yeah?" Traxler said.

"I can." I knelt beside the body, opening the sturdy leather bag that accompanied me on such missions and plucking the surgical scissors from their pouch within. I was sure that Traxler would be pleased the killing took place in the bathroom. The cleansing of the area after my visit would be his task and not mine, and such organic detritus is always easier to remove from ceramics than it is carpet.

I removed the dead man's shoes and socks and tossed them aside. "Fetch the bags."

By the time he'd returned to the bathroom with a roll of strong plastic sacks, the surgical scissors had made short work of the corpse's clothing, so that I might dismember him unobstructed. Traxler shifted the body and yanked the slit garments from beneath depositing them in the sacks.

I replaced the scissors and delved further into my bag to find the pouch of bone cutters. The instruments clicked gently together as I unrolled the pouch on the cold bathroom floor. My fingers hovered over the bound tools for a moment or two, as if selecting a dessert, passing over the rongeur and the Gigli wires, and eventually settling on the unsubtle majesty of a simple hacksaw.

I began, as always, with the feet.

Perhaps because of my own patchwork genesis, I am exquisitely comfortable with disjecta membra. It reminded me of pornography, faceless, cultivating intimacy and remoteness at the same time, humanity devolved to fleshy segments. The repetitive back and forth of the saw is as workmanlike as the passionless thrusts of the performers on the screen.

It wasn't long before my blade hit bone and I steadied myself, putting a little more weight behind the saw. I felt Traxler watching me, his eyes intense upon my flexing shoulders. He desired me, I knew, but such a coupling was repulsive to me. I shrieked in the face of my first unwanted suitor and his brutish urges, and have done so many times since, my screams evolving from ones of terror to those of rage.

At last, both feet were detached, ankles frayed with ruffs of tendon, stark masts of bone jutting from meat like the stiff tails of kittens. Once Traxler had added them to a bag of their own, I started sawing below the knees.

Traxler's attention meant little to me. My aesthetics are my own, not some contrived lure for the gaze of others. My hair retains the fiery hue of its creation, and though I sport a shorter, more convenient style now, I've always kept the bold, pale lightning streaks that sweep from my temples. Traxler, and many more men and women over the decades, have presumed the streaks to be an affectation, and I've never cared enough to explain how they honour the ignition of my birth.

The sutures binding my flesh together have long since turned to dust, but the pale scars of my creator's inelegant stitches remain, submerged now beneath a glory of tattoos. Expediently, the ink draws less questions than the scarring, but I will confess a certain vanity in how I chose the tattoos to tell something of my history. Deciphered, the ink would tell of a witch and a wartime assassin, a housekeeper and a princess and a private detective, a dozen lifetimes. My first tattoo, faded now but long-treasured, ran along the scar above my heart: *We Belong Dead*.

"I've been meaning to ask," Traxler said as I continued sawing. "What do you do with the parts? I mean, obviously you get rid of them, but how? Furnace? A big bath of acid?"

I prised back a kneecap for purchase. "We live in a world of secrets, Traxler. You should consider my methods as one of them."

"Well, forgive me for fucking breathing." He pouted, taking first one shin from me, then the other, and dropping them into a bag. "There's no need to be oversensitive about it."

Both legs were severed now. Then the hands, the arms, and finally, the broken blister of the dead man's skull. Traxler's gloved hand held it by the ear and dropped it into one of the sacks. Four sacks in total, a fifth when we bagged the torso.

Traxler took the heaviest of the sacks to my car, leaving me with my own leather bag and the refuse sack containing the hands, feet and head. Outside, we piled the grim mountain of segments into the boot of my car, and I slipped my leather bag onto the passenger seat.

Traxler lit a cigarette, taking a brief respite before he went to fetch the cleaning materials from his own vehicle.

"Oh yeah, I almost forgot," he said. "Mr. Dillon said to tell you he's got a business meeting next week. Three bodies, maybe four, depending on how the negotiations go. You up for that?"

I slid into the driver's seat. "He has my number. But tell him . . . " I started the engine. "Tell him I'll be charging extra for anything *disorderly*."

Traxler said something more, but his words were lost in the song of the engine as I drove away.

The factory was on the edge of town, long abandoned and encircled by a rusting chainlink fence, the barrier broken by a padlocked gate to which I have the only key. I parked in shadows and took the sacks of corpse meat from the boot.

Without, the factory was crumbling stone and decades-old graffiti. Within, it was a maze of warped floors and malformed staircases, buckled ceilings and lightless passageways. A labyrinth treacherous enough to deter even the most daring of urban explorers, but I knew it well enough to navigate my way through its channels to the long, wide workshop at its centre.

Machinery still loomed there, the rusted monoliths of some dead industry. I strode between them, past conveyor belts buried inches deep in dust and the corroded contraptions of gears and gauges that sprouted from concrete like steel tumours, until I reached the pit.

The pit was broad and deep, its curved walls lined with concrete. Metres above it was a long-rusted hatch, and I imagined that there had once been a connecting pipe of some kind, that the pit was the vent of a kiln, perhaps. In my initial explorations, I'd found that it branched off into several conduits of various sizes, all of them sealed at the furthest end with a steel grate. There was no way out, but a blackened steel service ladder clung to the interior walls of the pit, and should he have wished to, my companion could come and go as he pleased, staying within the confines of the factory for safety and discretion.

As I approached the edge, my shoes beat a gentle tattoo in the plaster dust, and from the darkness I heard the rustle of a blanket disturbed, the shuffle of naked feet upon stone. I looked within, and glimpsed a grey sliver of his brow as he drew forward.

"Friend?" His voice echoed from the pit, low and rasping, stale air across vocal cords like scorched leather.

*Friend.* He says little else these days, which feels apt, as we have little else but the simple love of friendship to entwine us. Like me, he is a living tapestry, stitched together into his own glorious gestalt. I have no knowledge of where his many pieces originated, nor does it matter, as Friend is as good a name for him and his good, purloined heart as any.

"Yes," I told him. "Yes, it's me."

I lifted the first of the bags, the one containing the head, hands and feet, and knelt, offering the sack into the shadows. I would not feed him as an animal, tossing bones and meat into his domain to pluck from the dirt. He was neither pet nor captive.

No chains bound him to the pit, save perhaps the chains of misplaced shame. He deemed his countenance monstrous, a jigsaw assembled by a maniac, its terrain made ever more exotic by the great swathes of scar tissue that shrouded his broken features. He protected me, that first night, shielded my body from the flames with his own, but at a terrible cost, his own body blackened and burned.

He has no place in a world of beauty, he once said, but in the factory, there is a small window that faces east, and there are nights when I return to find his broad footprints in the dust, a trail to the window and back to the pit, and I know that he has watched the sun rise or set.

Now his hands rose from the gloom of the pit, grey as ash on the hearth, nails silted with filth, knuckles as rugged as a mountain range. Long fingers, as if they once belonged to a pianist, enfolded the sack in my own hands and drew it back, into the darkness.

"Foooood . . . " he growled, one of the few other words he would utter. I heard more shuffling as he withdrew, then the rending of plastic as he freed his sustenance. A pause, while he appraised it, then a hard, sudden thud, followed by a thick, liquid chewing. He'd begun his feast with the head, it seemed.

I stepped away to let him eat in peace, leaving the other bags at the edge of the pit for later. Friend was apt to devour whatever was placed before him, hurriedly, like a famished man who fears when he might dine again, and so I took it upon myself to regulate his consumption. This saddened me.

As the decades turned and my own intellect flourished, he gradually became afflicted with some dreadful derangement of the senses, something akin to a mortal dementia. Once, long ago, his manner was as noble as his inhuman nature allowed, seeking only the virtuous ideals of love and companionship, and in that sense, I owe my existence as much to him as I do to the hands of crazed science. Yes, his attention had been unwanted, but he has saved me from flames and baying mobs, and I am indebted to him for that if nothing else. That was why I chose to keep him safe, away from this world of temptations and betrayals.

I crossed to one of the scarred wooden workbenches and sat, opening one of the textbooks I kept here for my visits. I know not the cradle of cold bone my brain came from, but my mind is a fine one, soaking up equations and principles and formulae with ease. I sometimes ponder that had I not had to hide Friend's existence and my own, I might have unlocked scientific secrets of which my creator could only have dreamed.

Some time passed, and at last I set down my book and rose to lower another bag into the pit. It was then I heard the noise, the clatter of metal upon metal, some fallen pipe clattering down a staircase, perhaps. I turned in the direction of the sound, drawing back my overcoat to let my fingers rest upon the holster at my hip.

I held my breath, listening to the approaching footfalls, a gait I recognised even before I saw the tall, slim silhouette emerging from one of the interior doors.

"Whoa there, Annie Oakley," Traxler said, smiling. "Stow the iron. I come in peace."

My fingers relaxed but did not move. "What are you doing here? You have no business in this place."

"Well . . . " He scratched at the thin stubble of his jaw. "I think the better question is what are *you* doing here? This is where you bring the bodies, yeah? But . . . " he glanced around. "I'm not seeing anything like a furnace or an acid bath. What are you doing with them? Just . . . burying them? Mr. Dillon won't be too happy knowing there's a bunch of corpses ready to be dug up one day."

"There are no corpses buried here, Traxler,' I said. "Not yet."

He laughed, gesturing at my sidearm. "No need to be hostile. This is just a friendly visit."

I let my overcoat fall forward over the holster once more. I would learn more from him if I allowed him the pleasure of explaining it to me. "You followed me." I prompted.

"Well, yes and no." He shrugged. "I *have* followed you here, a couple of times. First time I've popped in for tea, though."

"No corpses, and no tea," I said quietly. "Leave. Now."

"I will, I will." He entered the great hall of the workspace on the opposite side of the pit to where I stood, and I was grateful for the distance it enforced. He edged forward to glance into the depths, pausing only to spit experimentally into the darkness before smiling at me once more. "But let's talk first. It doesn't look like you get much company around here. You might even enjoy it."

"I won't." My rage at his intrusion, at his presumption, uncoiled with reptile grace in the centre of me. "Go."

He reached into his jacket and my fingers tensed once more, until he pulled out his pack of cigarettes and a lighter. "Y'know," he muttered around the filtertip. "You're not like any woman I've ever met. You're tough, smart. It's intriguing." He snapped his lighter shut and tucked it away. "Even kind of sexy."

"I don't care for your cigarette smoke in here any more than I care for anything else of your presence," I said. "Go now. Talk to Dillon if you must but leave this place."

He let a thin cloud of grey leak from his lips before replying. "Look, I'm sorry I followed you, okay? I told you I was just curious, and if you hadn't been so weird back in the bathroom, I wouldn't have had to poke my nose in."

He walked as he spoke, circling the pit between us, moving closer with each careful step. "The other blokes talk about you, y'know. They think you're weird, what with the scars and the ink and that thing you do with your hair, the, uhm." He gestured vaguely. "The lightning thing."

"The idle prattle of you and your associates means nothing to me," I hissed, watching as he took another step nearer.

"Oh, don't get me wrong, I don't join in with them or anything. I like how you look."

I snorted at words meant as a balm. So predictable. I had stated *my* feelings and his instinctive response was to volunteer *his*.

He was closer now though, still skirting the great mouth of the pit but advancing even as he spoke again. "You're not like other women, and I'm not like those other blokes. I promise you. I'm a nice guy."

"You are a liar," I said. "You are *precisely* the same as them. You see nothing of me beyond the flesh. Only breasts, a sex, a mouth to serve or praise you."

He chuckled forth a jet of cigarette smoke. "Sounds good to me."

"Our discourse is over," I said, reaching to my hip and drawing my sidearm. The pistol was small, but Traxler's eyes still widened a little. He raised his palms, not in surrender, but in placation.

"Hey, hold on there, sweetheart. There's no need for that." His hands still raised, he flicked his cigarette away. It darted into the shadows like a shooting star.

"I am *more* than just parts, Traxler," I whispered, and felt that mighty rage, the one born of a scream on a stormy night, tighten its embrace on my innards. It felt good. "But if you wish so dearly to learn my secrets, then let the lesson begin."

Logic tells us to aim for the torso, the largest scope of the body, to pierce a major organ, perhaps twist even the heart itself to offal. I aimed for where Traxler kept his brains, and his crotch dissolved in a thick mist of red. He crumpled, his shrieks an agreeable echo within the factory walls.

I crossed to him. His jacket had fallen open, revealing his own sidearm tucked beneath his armpit, and I reached forward to pluck the weapon from its holster. He snatched uselessly at me with one gore-gloved hand; the other still clutched the wreckage of his genitals, his pulped penis and scrotum squeezing through his fingers like a soft, porous pudding. A great pond of blood was spreading beneath him; its expanding edge trembled at the brim of the pit and trickled over.

From the darkness of the pit, I heard movement.

I tossed his pistol aside, heard it clatter forever out of his reach, but still Traxler swung his clutching hand at me. The cords in his neck stood taut as piano wire. His eyes burned, and frothing white flowers of saliva blossomed at the corners of his mouth.

"You fucking *whore*!" he snarled, punctuating his invective with a thick, agonised growl. "You fucking *bitch*!"

I'd heard the words many times; pain or fear robs even the most eloquent of men of all but the basest of vocabulary, and the slurs no longer held any power for me. I glanced at his ruptured crotch; what might have been his glans peeped between his fingers, the bulb engorged with blood even as its eye drizzled red.

My leather bag was still on the passenger seat, with its pouch of bone cutters. Traxler would die, of course, but I thought that I could keep him alive long enough for him to know which limbs were being severed.

*I come in peace*, he'd said, and it amused me to think he might leave in pieces.

He was still ranting, but again I heard movement in the pit, a creak of straining metal. A motion caught my eye and I saw that the top of the service ladder that poked above the lip of the pit was trembling. A grunt from below accompanied each quiver, a grunt and a tinny squawk as decades-old rungs yielded beneath his footfalls.

Friend was ascending.

Traxler could hear him too, and he craned his head back to look at the quaking ladder. "What the . . . what the fuck is that? Wha—" His last words devolved into another liquid gasp of anguish. He writhed beside the pit like a skewered insect.

The great dome of Friend's skull rose from the pit, his face mostly hidden by the tangled beard that sprouted from it and the mane of iron-grey hair that shrouded his brow. I could see his eyes, though. They were blue, bluer than I remembered, and sadder.

He drew himself a little higher, his torso arcing from the blackness, and my heart broke to see his ashen shape, the wilted sacs of his chest and the corrugated terrain of his ribcage, a man of bones bound together by scar tissue. He lifted a shaking hand, extending one long finger to point at Traxler's squirming form.

"Friend?"

"No, my dear," I said. "Food."

"Foooood . . . " he breathed, his scabbed lips twitching into a smile. He stretched forth a sinewy arm, his fingers entangling themselves in Traxler's thick hair. Traxler shrieked, his hands flying from his ravaged genitals to batter uselessly at Friend's grip, and with his free hand Friend began to clamber back down the ladder, dragging Traxler with him.

Traxler slid along the brim of the pit, his unravelled testicles trailing between his legs like fleshy streamers, until Friend leapt the last few feet to the ground, and Traxler's body flipped limply into the gloom.

By the time his screams ceased, the night was almost over.

I sat at the edge of the great, dark cave where Friend had been entombed, and decided that once he finished dining, I would seek to coax him from the blackness. Through one of the factory's broken windows, the one that faced east, the first glimmers of dawn were touching the horizon, and if he was willing, I hoped we might see the sun rise together.

Arlo Gorevin lives in the UK, thrives primarily on energy drinks, and is owned by two potentially demonic cats. His work has appeared in *Hellhound Magazine*, the *Cosmos Hundred Word Horror* Anthology from Ghost Orchid Press, the *666 Dark Drabbles* Anthology from Black Hare Press, the *Welcome to The Splatter Club Vol 2* Anthology from Blood Bound Books and the *Books of Horror Community Anthology Volume 4*. Every time he writes his bio, he imagines it's his obituary.

THE FOLLOWING STORIES
ARE THE GROSS-OUT
CONTEST WINNERS FROM
AUTHOR CON II
WILLIAMSBURG, VA 2023

# LICK YOUR FINGERS

## AuthorCon II Gross Out Winner

## Chris DiLeo

THIS IS WHAT happens when you're not yet a year old, but you can crawl and today you're in the bathroom.

There's a fresh treat in the cat box.

It's slick, wet and glistening, and almost slips from your fingers. The smell is pungent sweet and you bite into it, a long, mushy clump of cat shit. Little crunchy bits squish to ash. The shit smears all over your teeth and tongue. You lick it off your fingers.

At the toilet, you pull yourself up, try to reach for the water. The seat is wet. You slide your hands across it. Smells like piss. You lick each palm.

You slip, fall, and crawl behind the toilet where it's slimy and you can taste the sticky underside of the bowl.

There's clumpy goop on the plunger. You peel it off and suck it into your mouth. It's mushy.

The toilet brush is prickly, but there's water in its holder. You pick it up. Dark things float in it. You drink. It splashes on your face and you smear it all into your mouth.

You look around. Ah, the trash can.

You spill it out around you.

So many tissues.

Hard pebbles of snot and gooey pustules of phlegm. You chew and swallow. Slivers of Daddy's toenails, clippings hard and pointy and stab your throat.

There's a dead cockroach you grab and its little legs twitch. You want to giggle, the way it walks inside your mouth.

Crunch. Its insides spit goo. Yum.

One of your soggy diapers is next, but you can't unwrap it—squeezing, though, it makes squelchy sounds and you lick at the dribbles of runny, green seepage.

You don't know what the next thing is, but it looks tasty—like a cherry-flavored ice pop, except its cottony soft with a long dangling string.

It smells fruity and sweet and a little bit fishy.

Licking only makes it stick to your tongue, so you bite it and chew and chew. Juice seeps out. It's metallic and salty and swells your mouth all puffy.

You spit it out, see what's next.

A thing you tug and stretch between your hands, rubbery and funny the snappy sounds it makes.

It's sweaty and moist, oniony and seaweed-pungent, and it's very, very chewy. It slips around in your mouth. You chew and chew. Something salty oozes onto your tongue. You squeeze the nipple-like end sagging against your chin, and splooge squirts out of it into the back of your throat.

It's salty and creamy and gooey and soapy and thick like phlegmy-mucus, wetly thwacking your throat, sticking there.

You try to swallow, can't.

You push the whole rubbery thing further with your small fingers and swallow, swallow, swa—

It's stuck. You gag. Can't breathe. Your face flushes hot.

You pull at it, stretching it, but it's glued to your throat.

Mommy opens the door, sees you, your face crimson and purplish-blue, throat engorged, a used condom stretching from your mouth like a second tongue.

She yanks you from behind the toilet, her hands slipping on your slimy skin, and she fishhooks fingers in your mouth. The rubber thing rips free and you can breathe again as Mommy puts you down, her face paling, she falls to her knees going for the toilet but liquidy globs plop from her mouth and splat on the floor.

It smells acidic but it looks warm, and Mommy is gasping as she turns to see you scoop a yellowy-orange clump of puke off the floor and slurp it between your lips.

This time, Mommy pukes in the toilet.

You listen to the splashes and lick your fingers clean.

Chris DiLeo is the author of numerous books, most recently *The Hands of Onan* from Grindhouse Press about a writer who must infiltrate an all-male masturbation cult to save his friend. Of that book, Amazon reviewers have said it is "suspenseful and funny as hell," "exciting and surprisingly thoughtful," "fun, snappy, gross," "darkly funny," "compulsively readable," and "a sublime piece of dark fiction." DiLeo's AuthorCon Gross-Out-winning story, "Lick Your Fingers," was his first entry into the contest and he hopes one day to repeat his championship performance. He lives in New York, teaches high school English, and writes in an office with multiple cats and two book-filled coffins. He is online as @authordileo.

# EYE OF THE HOLDER, A PARABLE

## LUCAS MILLIRON

**Y**OU EVER NUT in a condom, then leave it on in case you need to use it again? Leave it on, say, a month? Maybe two, maybe a year? That's what it's like sleeping in your contact lenses.

Might not have been Casey's first time sleeping in her contacts, but it was the first time Ms. Anthony noticed the corneal ulcer on her one real eye was oozing. Her eyelid looked like a hooker's twat after a creampie train. Puss dripped down her cheeks, and blood vessels invaded the body of the contact lens. She lit a cigarette and picked the pussy orbit in front of the mirror.

With its open sores and weeping blisters, Casey's face was the texture of pomegranate seeds. Her fingers groped a swollen, sticky spot on her upper lip the size of a grape. She pinched, scratching it till it popped. More puss cascaded down her lips, looking and tasting like warm almond milk.

Ms. Anthony's tongue found the open sore, tasting the salt under her skin like a busted nut. Licking the wound like a hot clit, she noticed a smell of old mayonnaise and strong cheese. She looked around, checked the bottom of her feet to make sure she hadn't stepped in dog shit.

Casey smacked her forehead when she remembered what the odor was. She dug her thumb under her false eye and pried it out of its socket. She dropped it into her palm and looked it over. The back side of the prosthetic was caked with globs of golden eye cheese. The sticky, gritty substance reeked of old milk and rotting pumpkin.

Casey flicked the cheese off with her finger, then tossed the false eye in her mouth. She swished the prosthetic with her tongue, savoring the sweat, gritty flavors of goat cheese and Miracle Whip, then spat it out in her hand.

Ms. Anthony licked her fingers for lubricant and shoved it back in place, blinking a few times to make sure it was good and settled, then checked the time on her phone. She was late for her appoint with Aaron. Ms. Anthony scratched her muff and sniffed her fingers. Her nails reeked of skunky beer, apple cider vinegar, and pennies. She corked her red snapper with a fresh tampon, then got dressed to meet her plug.

Aaron's scrawny, tatted ass wasn't perturbed by the red tide, oh no. After smoking meth behind the Dunkin' Donuts dumpster, Aaron pulled out Casey's tampon with his teeth, dropped the vampire tea bag in his mouth, then pulled out as if it were edamame. He smiled like a red-lipped clown before raw dogging her beef curtains.

Aaron's ten-inch gooey duck was stained orange, a commingling of menses and yeasty fluids. He cocked back his scrawny, crackhead pelvis, then slammed his hips hard into her ass, gasping when his nut sack slapped her creamy cunt. The impact knocked out Casey's false eye and teeth with a wet *slurp*.

While Casey reached for her spare parts, Aaron slammed her peanut butter cooter again. This time, she felt a pop as the cornea tore on her "good eye." Vitreous fluids oozed from under the contact as her eye deflated like a squished grape.

Everything vanished in a haze of blurry, searing pain.

"Not again!" Casey bawled.

You've only got two eyes, and sometimes, you're lucky enough to have that.

Lucas Milliron is a born and raised native Floridian, oldest of three siblings to a loving mother and father. Married to his wife, he still resides in South Florida as a Licensed eye care professional. Lucas Milliron, Weird Florida Fiction.

# A MOIST DAY AT THE POOL

## LUCY LEITNER

THE AIR WAS thick as smegma. You expect a certain moistness in a warm Virginia summer day at the pool, but the moistness was moistening my skin even more than whatever pestilence was coursing within me could possibly moisten. Though my mom didn't believe it when she forced me to attend swim practice, the phlegm was building up in my throat, the mucus threatening seepage from my nose. I imagined it bubbling between the lane markers, clouding the water, forming some sort of super-snot that was impervious to the chlorine.

Maybe that's how I had contracted my ailment, from the sputum bubbles the other kids were splooging into the pool. In my eleven-year-old mind, clotted yolk-like secretions floated through the lanes, oozing into the nasal passages of my teammates, coagulating into a pulp in the clefts above their lips. It would later dry into a crust their mothers would have to scrape from their tender flesh, almost like penance for forcing them to practice when they should have been lying flaccid on the couch for as long as it took to squelch the infestation from their bodies.

Thus, my throat engorged with what could only be the larval stage of a corpuscle-filled goiter, I approached the eight-lane pool. The sun was little more than a veiny protrusion among the dense clouds that emitted the slightest tinkle of liquid, leaving my skin damp and glistening. A fresh wave of queasiness wriggled through me.

Was it the sky's renal activity or the boy, about my age as far as I could tell, squatting above a soggy puddle on an otherwise barren pool deck?

With squeamish fascination, I watched his tofu flesh jiggle oh so slightly as he sat, crotch first, in the puddle.

I couldn't help noticing the way his pubescent gullet dangled over his Speedo that clung like panties over his pubis when he lifted one of his lard-colored legs at a right angle, plunging his foot into his maw.

He suckled on the big toe. *Slurp, slurp, slurp* quickly gave way to *munch, munch, munch.* His jowls jiggled, viscous saliva dripping from his mouth as he bit into the fungus-ridden toenail. Popped blisters from the rough pool deck speckled the bottom of his raised foot, fetid pus oozing from the sloughed skin. But the boy didn't care. The mayonnaise-like substance slid down his flaccid chest, leaving it wet and speckled as hummus.

He masticated the toenail like it was gristle, smearing the milky discharge from whatever was living at the end of his foot to his orifice. He continued to munch, not only devouring the toenail, but the pustule on the inner side of the toe, leaving a gash in the skin to fester in its putrescence. The seepage from this new wound was wretched. No ointment could prevent it from forming a fetid scab. Licking the crevices between protuberances, his tongue thrusting over each papule, he lapped up any remaining carbuncles.

His hand behind his neck, elbow pointed to the sky, he inhaled the ripe stench of his moist armpit. What looked like amputated nubs of cysts dribbled from his nose. He flapped his grubby hands, smiled to reveal a colony of wriggling roaches between the pronged teeth, content with his grotesque meal as if he were a slobbering pug after devouring raw giblets. Tilting his head back, he gargled, and began ululating with such volume the splashing in the pool stopped.

As the boy belched, a thick, opaque substance not unlike larva squirted from his mouth. Gushing, the gooey spunk impregnated the soupy, ever-moistening air with the sulfurous odor of unruly flatulence.

The feculent stench, the smeared leakage congealing on his cheeks, and the way his belly jiggled and engorged from his autophagous feast were too much for my already squeamish eleven-year-old body to take.

My face turning puce, I ran from the lap pool to my mother and sister in the baby pool, reaching it just in time to spew chunks of a porridge-like color and consistency into the shallow water. The curds of my vomit separated in the pool, like maggots, the mushy expulsion threatening to clog the drains. I gurgled as the last of the yeasty substance and the nausea left my body.

See, mom, I was sick.

Lucy Leitner is the author of *Influence: #horrorstories, Bad Vibrations, Outrage: Level 10, Nemesis Selection, Working Stiffs,* and an unpublished *Shrek* rip-off she wrote and illustrated as an eight-year-old. She lives in Pittsburgh, PA.

# TEETH

## MEGAN STOCKTON

THIS WASN'T AN ideal situation.

Let's be honest though, she hadn't been in an *ideal situation* in thirty years, but this really took the fucking cake. One moment she was in her favorite bar, hustling her favorite type of man: those weaselly, greasy scumbags that talked a big game and were happy to throw money at any pretty girl that acted a little too tipsy to have good judgment. Unfortunately, the intense pursuit caused her to lose track of her drink for just a little too long . . .

And now she woke up on the cool slick stone of a basement floor, illuminated only by the butter-yellow light of a single, bare bulb on the ceiling. This had to have been his house, but she didn't know who he was yet.

As though he'd heard the cue for his entrance, the door across the room opened. The man that entered was a gelatinous heap of hairy, liver-spotted rolls. His calves were thicker than his feet, excess flesh hanging down just above his heels. He both looked and felt heavy, walking through the room and bringing with him a warmth and dampness to the air. He waddled toward her, panting through his chapped lips. It wasn't until he stepped beneath the solitary bulb that she noticed he was also naked. A generous flab of jiggling tissue fell over his groin and completely obscured any sight of his dick. *Thank God.*

She sat up slowly, head aching, teeth on fire. She touched a damp welt on the back of her skull from where this guy or an accomplice struck her. Blood-matted hair stuck to her fingers. They were idiots if they thought she was going down easy.

He stepped before her and looked down, fat rolls compressing his windpipe, forcing him to wheeze.

"Now, you're going to be a good girl, aren't you?" he struggled to say, spittle flying from his plump lips and draining down his chin. He wagged a sausage-finger at her and she nodded, putting on her best doe eyes and parting her lips to take in a faux-terrified gasp. He scratched beneath one of his skin folds, cheesy-white clumps sticking underneath his overgrown nails. Every rake across his skin conjured a new wave of stench: a marriage of sweet rot and cat piss.

He waded through the mass of wiry, gray pubic hair, and she cringed as small insects skittered against the flakey skin there. Their bodies were nearly translucent: digestive tracts full of shit and blood were visible, squiggly highways in their abdomens. When he lifted his stomach to give better sight of his small penis, she noted that it was scabby and oozing, and smelled remarkably like the time a mouse had died against the heating element in her apartment's dryer.

"Put it in your mouth," he said, snorting as yellow-snot poured out of his nose and a snail-trail of pre-cum struggled to dribble around a gnarly scab on the head of his dick.

She licked her lips and crawled forward on her hands and knees, breath held because retching and dry heaving against the floor wasn't sexy last she checked. She put *just the tip* in her mouth, barely closing her lips around what little shaft wasn't buried in adipose.

He shuddered at the contact.

And then she bit down.

Her teeth clamped together so forcefully her ears rang. She shook her head from side to side like a dog, until the tissue tore away. The man stumbled backward, arms pin-wheeling as he tried to catch himself before falling to the floor.

It wasn't a long fall for him, his portly form bouncing against the pavement as he rolled like an over-inflated ball, reaching down to clutch his spurting groin.

She gasped, having forgotten she was holding her breath this whole time, and subsequently sucked the man's amputated dick down her throat.

It barely cleared her tongue before catching in her windpipe. For a terrifying moment she couldn't breathe, her face grew hot and her lungs burned for oxygen. Then she managed to huff the tiniest amount of air through his piss hole—no doubt obscured by that crusty scab she'd spied earlier.

She calmed down, taking small breaths in and out, the scab flapping back and forth like an unreliable epiglottis.

Note to self: length don't matter, girth don't matter. If you're going to bite off a dick, make sure his piss hole is big enough to breathe through.

The man continued to roll on the floor, his naked body turning blue as he uttered something along the lines of *you stupid fucking cunt.*

She needed to get to a bathroom so she could hack up this dick and use some Listerine to sanitize. She stumbled across the floor, slipping in a puddle and falling briefly alongside her captor. He'd shit himself apparently, and now she was sitting bare assed in a soured diarrheal stew. She got up, gagging but unable expel the vomit. It backed up in her throat and she fought to swallow it down, while tiny amounts of $O_2$ whistled through the musty air hole of life.

She wiped her hands on her thighs, smearing grainy yellow shit across her skin as she headed straight for the simple staircase. She ascended with caution, but when she saw the front door of the old farmhouse on the upper level she picked up the pace.

From an adjacent room, a scrawny, bald-headed man emerged with a skillet in his hand, striking her across the jaw with all the might his little stature could muster.

She saw stars, and several of her pearly-whites clattered across the floor like rogue dice. On the positive side of things, it also dislodged the head of the dick from her throat. She gasped in relief, watching the blunt chunk of sausage sail through the air.

The man pulled a pair of pliers out of his pocket, grinning as he approached. "Ain't going to have to worry about biting when I get done with you."

Staggering in the newfound delirium of the blow, she braced herself against the wall, and snarled: "I don't need any fucking teeth."

Megan Stockton is an indie author who lives in Grimsley Tennessee with her two children and her husband, who is an indie filmmaker. She writes in a variety of genres that all have dark/horror elements, and all of her work is character-driven and immersive. She is known for delivering works that are raw, thought-provoking, brutal, and cinematic. She has been writing since she was a child and was always obsessed with horror and the macabre. When she isn't writing (or working her day job) she likes to work with the animals on their farm, read, play video games, and watch movies.

# ABOUT THE EDITOR

Nikki Noir writes erotic thrillers, extreme horror, and bizarre plot-lines. Her fiction can be found on Blood Bound Books. Her visual art and love of all things spooky can be found at At That Spooky Beach on IG and TikTok.

Join Blood Bound Books Newsletter for updates and to receive 20% off your next order at www.BloodBoundBooks.com

**Artist Corlen Scope teamed up with author Kristopher Triana to bring you the most insane adult coloring book on the market! Featuring 35 graphic images,** *Body Art—The Coloring Book* **brings the pages of the best-selling novel to life.**

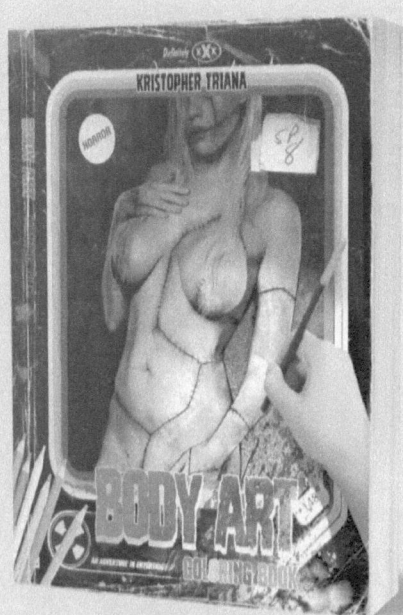

# "ON JUNE 6TH, 2006, THREE FRIENDS ENTERED A PACT WITH A SUCCUBUS. MUSICAL FAME AND FORTUNE WOULD BE THEIRS PROVIDED THE WOMEN COULD FULFILL THE DEMON'S NEED FOR SEXUAL ENERGY WITH WILLING SPIRIT SPOUSES.

## BOTH PARTIES AGREED, AND SUCK-U-BUS WAS BORN."

That's what the website claimed. But it was just a gimmick to sell tickets. Or so Lisa Hummer thought.

After her brother gets a backstage bus-pass, she isn't so sure. A strange woman warns them the succubus has marked Danny for more than sex, and it isn't long before Danny goes missing.

Following the clues, Lisa uncovers a trail of chaos wherever the band plays. She can't be certain if there is a nefarious plot or if it's simply a bizarre series of coincidences.

Is the succubus real or is it all in her head?

There's something under your bed.

It hates you. It wants to devour you and everyone you love.

Dad's at work. Mom's dead drunk and no help whatsoever.

Maybe your stuffed rabbit can help, since he seems to be alive and talking now. Then again, maybe that just means you've finally gone around the bend.

Whatever plan you come up with to survive the night, though, you'd better not let so much as a fingertip stray off your mattress. If you do, you'll be ripped to bloody chunks by...

mybook.to/TTU

WHEN ONE MAN
INFILTRATES AN ALL-
MALE MASTURBATION
CULT, THINGS GET
OUT OF HAND.

@authordileo

# NO GUTS, NO GLORY HOLE!

Toxic Love is a darkly comedic and erotic nightmare from the master of blood-soaked horror, Kristopher Triana. Throughout this tale of perversion, gore, and gangsters, Triana pens powerful characters who will move you just as deeply as they'll repulse you.

THIS IS A WILDLY ENTERTAINING,
FUNNY, AND DARK NOVELLA ABOUT A
MAN AND HIS ALIEN PARASITE WHO
LIVES IN HIS
BRAIN.

READ NOW :

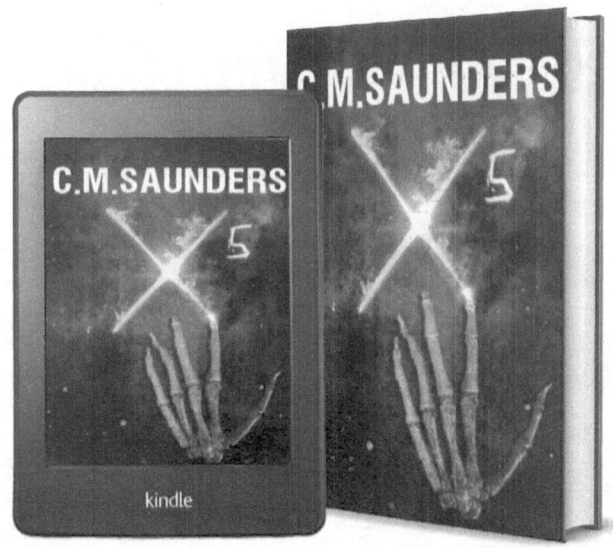

Meet the local reporter on an assignment which takes him far beyond the realms of reality, join the fishing trip that goes sideways when a fish unlike any other is hooked, and find out the hidden cost of human trafficking in China. Along the way, meet the hiker who stumbles across something unexpected in the woods, the office worker whose life is inexorably changed when a medical drug trial goes wrong, and many more.

# Some things should never be consumed...

"It's like watching an episode of Ash Vs. the Evil Dead."

– Sci-Fi & Scary

"If you want extreme horror that can deliver powerful character development while still making you cringe, come get your freak on!"

– Nikki Noir, Redrum Reviews

www.ingramcontent.com/pod-product-compliance
Lightning Source LLC
Chambersburg PA
CBHW021925170626
46807CB00007B/2987